FORGOTTEN VICTIM

An absolutely gripping crime mystery with a massive twist

HELEN H. DURRANT

Detective Rachel King Thrillers Book 4

JOFFE
BOOKS

First published 2020
Joffe Books, London
www.joffebooks.com

Join our mailing list and become one of 1,000s of readers enjoying free Kindle crime thriller, detective, mystery, and romance books and new releases. Receive your first bargain book this month!

www.joffebooks.com

We love to hear from our readers! Please email any feedback you have to: feedback@joffebooks.com

ISBN: 978-1-78931-644-5

PROLOGUE

Finn Kendal nudged his mate. "Do you believe in ghosts?"

"Don't be daft," Jack said.

"Well, my mum does. She reckons this place is haunted," Finn replied.

"Come on! You don't believe all that stuff, do you?"

"Dunno, but she's usually right."

Jack Handley shivered, his young eyes scouring the dark interior of the old mill for any glimmer of light. "It's bloody dark, I know that. And it stinks."

After years of decay and neglect, Shawcross Mill did indeed smell. The bags of rubbish which fly tippers had dumped in the yard didn't help either. None of that bothered Finn. To him, the disused and crumbling building was a great playground, a place to explore and ride his bike, away from the traffic.

He led Jack through the hole in the rear wall and into what had once been a huge weaving shed. "Isn't it great?" He smiled, waving his arms at the rusting spinning machines, dark hulks stacked in the shadows against the wall. "My grandad worked on them. Made his chest bad in the end." He crept over and ran his hand over an ancient loom, silent relic from a bygone age.

It was a sad end for a building that had once provided the livelihood for thousands. Shawcross dated from the days when cotton was king, and Manchester supplied the world. Not that the kids were interested in any of that, nor were they impressed by the rusting plaque on the wall proclaiming it to be one of the oldest mills in the area. To them it was an adventure playground, far more appealing than any park.

Every time he left the house, Finn's mother warned him not to go near the place. Her warnings fell on deaf ears. Finn had a mind of his own and, anyway, what could go wrong? He knew Shawcross like the back of his hand.

"Hear that noise?" Jack asked. "It *is* bloody haunted. Your mam was right."

Finn crouched down and pulled him closer to the wall. "That's no ghost, it's Spider — he uses this place for dealing. Keep your gob shut and he won't see us."

"*Spider*. That maniac? He's a violent bastard and he doesn't give a toss who he hurts. I'm not waiting around to get caught by him. Last week he slashed George's arm. Made a right mess." George was Jack's older brother.

"Shut it!" Finn hissed. "He's coming this way!"

A gruff voice called out into the gloom. "Who's there?"

"We need to move." Finn nudged his friend and together they crawled back towards the hole they'd just climbed through.

"Gotcha, you little shit! I'll teach you to spy on me." Spider yanked Finn to his feet.

"We weren't!" he screamed. "I thought the place were empty."

"What's happening?" shouted a second voice.

"Damn kids. I'll deal with them."

"They're only lads, Spider, let 'em go."

Finn felt the grip on his arm loosen. "Run!" he yelled to Jack.

The two boys scarpered, but not the way they'd come in. They headed off in the opposite direction, deeper into the mill, through the weaving shed and into a narrow corridor and then into another much smaller space. Rainwater had got in through the ceiling and the floor was wet. "Let's hide over there," Finn gasped. He dived behind a pile of boxes and skidded along the floorboards.

There was a loud crack as the rotten floor gave way under his weight. Screaming for help, Finn fell through into the darkness below.

"You okay?" Jack shouted. "I'll come down." He cast a quick glance behind — thankfully there was no sign of Spider. "Finn? You there?" There was no answer. "Finn!" he called again. "I'm trying to get down, grab my legs! Where are you? It's pitch black."

"Turn your phone on, div, get some light," Finn groaned.

Finn watched the light from Jack's phone cast eerie shadows on the walls as the other boy climbed down to him. The place was small — a cellar, perhaps? Finn hadn't been in here before, which was odd because he thought he'd explored every inch of the mill. "Ring your mum, get some help," he said.

Jack gave his mobile a shake. "There's no signal down here. Where are we anyway? It looks like some sort of cave."

Finn sat up, brushed himself down and looked around the strange little room. "Oh God. What's that smell?"

"It'll be rubbish. No one's been down here in years." Jack pointed to the brick walls. "Look at the size of them cobwebs."

"We've got to get out. That smell is doing my head in," Finn said.

Jack helped his mate to his feet and the pair of them crept around, feeling the walls, looking for a way out. "There's no door," Jack whispered, "and there's mud all over the floor. What is this place?"

"Dunno, but it stinks something awful," Finn said.

"Dead cat?" Jack suggested.

"How'd it get in?"

"Never mind that, how do we get out? We can't climb back up, there's nothing to stand on."

Finn took the phone, shone it around the walls and spotted an area where the brickwork was crumbling and masonry had fallen on to the floor. He raised his leg and gave it a kick. It didn't take much to send bricks and cement crashing down, revealing what looked like the entrance to a small tunnel. "The cat must have come in round the back somehow and squeezed in through there. Perhaps we could get out the same way."

"Leave it be," Jack said. "It could lead anywhere. We'll get lost."

But Finn wasn't listening. He was shining Jack's phone into the dark tunnel. "We should give it a go. What else do we do? We can't get out the way we got in."

Before Jack could stop him, Finn had shifted a few bricks and climbed through. "It's even smellier in here," he called back.

"Come out! It's dangerous. The ceiling might fall in on you."

"It's okay, Jack. I think I've found something to stand on. There's something in here we can use, it's a box or summat, but you'll have to help me drag it out." He moved towards a dark shape to one side of the tunnel.

Jack's voice was shaking. "What is it?" he asked.

Finn was fast losing it and very frightened. The tunnel was like a prison — narrow, dark, and there was that smell. He didn't do confined spaces and wanted out fast. "We have to get out, Jack."

Finn held Jack's phone aloft and screamed. On the floor were the remnants of a human body.

CHAPTER ONE

Tuesday

"What is this place?" DS Elwyn Pryce asked.

DCI Rachel King surveyed the dilapidated pile of bricks and wondered what it was still doing here. Similar buildings in Ancoats had been converted into swanky flats or flattened and the land built on. "Shawcross Mill." She pointed to the plaque on the rusting gate giving the date of the building. "Look at that. This is a piece of history, Elwyn. It's been here since the early nineteenth century. It must be one of the first mills in Ancoats."

Elwyn kicked a bag of rubbish out of the way. "Shame it's been left to rot, then. Shouldn't a building this old be listed or something, done up and kept for posterity?"

"It'd take a fortune to do that, and I believe it's still owned by the Shawcross family," she said. "Mathew Shawcross lives out near me somewhere. We'll be visiting, so you can ask him yourself why it's been left to go to wrack and ruin."

"Perhaps he's holding out for a developer to make him an offer. Most of the other mills in Ancoats have been snapped up and turned into flats. Have you seen the price of some of them?"

Rachel shot him a quizzical look. Was 'developer' an oblique reference to Jed McAteer, her long-time on-and-off love? She dismissed the thought almost as fast as it had occurred to her. Elwyn wasn't given to smart comments at her expense. "Again, too costly," she said. "Speaking of property, how's your search for a new home going?"

"I've decided to go for the one up the road from my sister," the Welshman told her. "It's a reasonable price, and now that Marie and me have split, it'll be plenty big enough."

A sensible decision, in Rachel's opinion. "Ffion will be able to keep an eye on you, make sure you eat properly."

"I don't want her wasting her time running after me. Ffion has her own life to lead."

"I'm sure she loves running after you, Elwyn. You're her baby brother. You're very lucky to have her."

They were met at the mill entrance by two figures in white forensic suits. Dr Judith Glover, a friend of Rachel's, known as Jude to the team, and her colleague, Dr Jason Fox.

"The air's a bit stale in there," Jude said, clearing her throat. "It's a bad one, worse than we first thought. He's been there a while, and there's not a lot left. He's mostly bones."

"Murder?" Elwyn asked. "Or is it some poor homeless bloke who bedded down for the night and died of hypothermia?"

"Definitely murder," Jude said. "He was sealed up in there, in a tunnel under the floor. I don't know exactly what killed him yet, but from the look of his knee joints, he could have been shot. I need to get him back and do the PM for that. But be warned, it'll take a while to get you anything useful."

Rachel felt a sudden rush of sympathy. "The poor man. Are you saying he was shot in the legs and left to die?"

Jude nodded. "It's a possibility. It looks to me as if he was left in the tunnel and then it was bricked up behind him. The bricks the boys broke through are more modern, and put in far more recently than the surrounding masonry."

The idea made Rachel squirm. "I can't imagine what he must have gone through, left like that to die in the dark and all alone."

"How d'you know it's a man?" Elwyn asked.

"His clothing," Jude said. "Granted, they're in tatters, but they're definitely a man's. One thing that might help, the body was lying on a pile of newspapers — possibly to mop up the blood if he was beaten prior to being shot. We'll take the lot to the morgue."

"Is there enough of the newsprint left to help with the timescale?" Rachel asked.

"If we're lucky, there might be a scrap we can decipher. I doubt his clothing will be of much help, it's pretty rotten, apart from a leather jacket. That is very distinctive and has an unusual design on the back. We might get something from the remains date-wise, but like I said, that'll take time. Oh, and there is something else." She held up an evidence bag. "A Saint Christopher pendant, solid gold with a chunky chain, held by his fingers."

"Like he'd snatched it from someone and died clutching it?"

"That's a possibility, Rachel, unless it's his. We'll run tests."

"Thanks, Jude. We'll have a look before you take him away."

Rachel and Elwyn negotiated the rubbish-strewn floor of the weaving shed and into the small room with the jagged hole in the floorboards. A ladder had been temporarily secured in place for the forensic people and Colin Butterfield, the pathologist, to gain access.

The ageing pathologist had just hauled himself out of the hole as they arrived. His heavy figure was easily recognisable despite the mask and overall. "I'm far too old for this malarkey," he complained. "It's a tricky one, Rachel, he's been dead a while, but we'll do our best."

Elwyn looked down the hole as the pathologist walked away. It was quite a drop. "Should you be clambering down there?" he said to Rachel. "What if you slip?"

"What d'you mean?"

With a quick glance around to ensure no one was listening, he nudged her. "Your condition, stupid. The baby."

She gave him a faint smile. Irrational as it was, she'd pushed all thoughts of the pregnancy to the back of her mind. She knew full well it was stupid. Her condition was a fact, and eventually the baby would be too. She could only stay in denial for so long. "Don't, Elwyn. I know you've got my best interests at heart but, please, just let me get on with the job."

"I'm only saying. You do need to be careful, you know."

"And I will be. Now stop it."

Elwyn Pryce was the only person who knew about Rachel's pregnancy, and that was how she wanted it to stay for now. Elwyn knew what an impulsive person she was. She made decisions on the spur of the moment that often seemed crazy to others, but she trusted her gut instinct, and usually was right to. She hadn't even told Jed McAteer, the child's father. "You go first. That way if I do fall, you'll act as a cushion."

"Cheeky."

They descended the ladder. The space was small, filthy. Rachel scanned the walls but couldn't see a door, just the hole in the ceiling they'd just climbed down and a gap in one of the walls which led off into a narrow, dark tunnel where the body lay. "What d'you reckon this place is?"

"It has to be part of the mill. It could be an old cellar, I suppose." He wheeled around, looking over the walls. "It looks like a place long forgotten. But this space and that tunnel must have had some function at one time."

"Whoever did this could have come and gone along there." She nodded at the tunnel. "Wonder where it leads?"

"It's pretty narrow and not very high. Quite a squeeze if you ask me."

One of the forensic investigators leaned down from above. "We think that space and that tunnel is something to do with the sewer system or the canal. We should be able to confirm it from the old plans of the city."

They'd do the research. There had to be a record somewhere. "I wonder who put him there? They must have already known the place." Rachel said to Elwyn. "Who found the body?"

"Two young lads. According to the officer they spoke to, they definitely didn't know about it. They live local and often play in the mill." Elwyn consulted his notebook. "Apparently, they were hiding from someone, did a runner and fell through the rotten floorboards. They found the tunnel looking for a way out, saw the remains and panicked."

"They must've been terrified." Rachel shuddered. "We'll speak to them later. Do we know what made them run? Who were they scared of?"

"Neither boy will say."

"It's quite deep in here and I can't get a phone signal, so how did they get out?"

"Anonymous call to the security firm that patrol the mill."

"They were lucky," Rachel said. "Without that call they could have been stuck here for days."

Rachel took a look at the body and her eyes filled with tears. Her emotions were getting the better of her — must be her topsy-turvy hormones. The man was mostly bones. His wrist was lying at a weird angle from his arm. His body was clothed but it had rotted and where the skin was exposed it had dried and hardened, particularly on his arms. Suddenly Rachel's head began to swim. "I'll have to go outside," she told Elwyn. "The air's not good in here and I'm starting to feel sick."

"Go easy. Don't trip over anything," he called after her.

Rachel knew he wouldn't stop the comments — he couldn't help himself. But sooner or later one of the team would notice the attention he was giving her and ask questions she didn't want to answer. Rachel wasn't yet ready to tell the world about the pregnancy. She hadn't made up her mind what she was going to do. If she was honest with herself, she didn't know. She needed time to think about it.

CHAPTER TWO

Finn Kendal and Jack Handley sat with their mothers in Finn's living room. A female PC was with them. Jack, the younger one, had smudges down his cheeks. He'd been crying. Rachel felt sorry for him.

She smiled at them. "It's okay, you haven't done anything wrong. We know you've had a scary time of it, but will you tell me and my colleague what happened?"

The boys looked at each other, as though not wanting to be the first to speak.

Better give them a bit of a nudge. "Okay, I'll start, then," Rachel said gently. "Jack, how old are you?" she asked.

"Eleven, miss."

"Finn?"

"Twelve. We were playing, that's all," he said defensively. "I wanted to show Jack where I ride my bike."

"I've told him that place is a death trap, but does he listen? Strong-willed little bugger he is. Does as he pleases, drives me mad," Finn's mother grumbled.

"Your mum's right," Rachel said. "Anything could happen to you in there. It's full of dangerous machinery." She waited, giving them time to settle. "Was anyone else in there with you? You told one of my officers you were in that room hiding."

"Yeah, but I don't know who it were. We heard voices and ran. Thought it might be a security guard or summat," Finn lied.

"It is important that you tell us everything," Rachel said. "We're trying to find out what happened to that man you found. Anything, no matter how small, might help."

His young face flushed. "He were dead, weren't he? Been there a while too." He hung his head. "We don't know owt."

"You're sure you're not scared of someone, or protecting a friend?"

The boys looked at each other and shook their heads. Rachel decided to leave it for now. They were upset and she didn't want to push it. She'd interview them again when they'd had chance to recover from the shock. She handed the boys' mothers her card. "If either of them wants to talk to me again, ring me."

But Finn's mother was angry. "Tell her the truth, Finn!" she snapped. "You know very well who else was in there. That waste of space, Spider, dealing his drugs!"

"Spider?" Elwyn queried.

"Dylan Healey. He lives over the road. His mother's never been able to do owt with him, lad's run wild since he was a nipper."

"Is this true, Finn?" Rachel asked.

The lad nodded. "He'll kill us for dobbing him in."

"He lays a finger on you and he'll have me to deal with," his mother said. "Thinks he runs these streets. Well, I'll show him."

"Someone alerted the security firm, told them you two were trapped," Rachel said. "If they hadn't, you might never have got out. That could well have been Spider."

Finn's mother stuck her nose in the air. "Well, if it was him, then it just goes to show there's some good in everyone."

"How long has the mill been shut?" Elwyn asked.

"It stopped being a cotton mill in my granny's time," Jack's mum said. "Since then loads of firms have tried their luck in the place. The owners divided it up into units and let them." She shook her head. "No one made much out of it, though. That old mill hasn't made money since the cotton days."

"Did your grandmother work there?" Elwyn asked.

"And my grandad," Jack's mum said. "Back in the day, so did most folk on these streets. Before the houses were bought out, they used to pay rent to the Shawcross family. Back in them days, lose your job and you lost your house too."

"What sort of businesses rented the units? Can you recall any of their names?" Rachel asked.

"There was all sorts. There was a sheet metal firm, but they didn't last. A car repair shop. There was that second-hand furniture bloke. Several of the units banded together and opened a craft market at one time. That was interesting — they sold pottery, handmade goods and other things. But it didn't last long either. Eventually they also gave up. Rents were high, not to mention the rates." Jack's mum shrugged.

"How long since the last business closed up and left?" Rachel asked.

"The car repair shop closed a couple of years ago."

"Do you remember what it was called?"

"Andy's Autos, I think. A young bloke called Andy Siddall ran it. He's still around somewhere," Jack's mum said, "but I don't know his address."

"This Dylan Healey, what number does he live at?" Rachel asked.

"Number fourteen, over th' road," said Finn's mother.

CHAPTER THREE

Rachel and Elwyn stood on the pavement outside Finn's house. Rachel looked up and down the narrow street of redbrick terrace houses. They'd been built for the mill workers, and were small, with shared backyards. Amid all the redevelopment that had taken place in Ancoats over the last decade, these streets represented a little bit of history the developers appeared to have missed.

"We'll have a word with Dylan Healey, aka Spider," Rachel said.

"If he's in," Elwyn added, and followed her across the road.

The front door was answered by a middle-aged man clutching a can of lager.

"He's out," he said.

Elwyn stuck his foot in the doorway. "Where's he gone?" he asked and showed the man his badge.

"Bloody coppers. Never leave the lad alone."

"Why's that, then? Naughty boy is he, your Dylan?"

The man nodded towards the stairs. "He's nowt to do with me, he's hers. But you can't talk to her cause she's in bed after her night shift. The lad is up the pub at the end of the street." He sneered. "Landlord won't be happy, you lot turning up. It'll give 'im a bad name."

Rachel called the station and spoke to Stella, one of the civilian information team. "Check the system for one Dylan Healey. He lives in Ancoats and he's a dealer, so I've been told."

"Okay, I'll ring you back when I've got something," Stella said.

Elwyn was looking at a sign above the pub window. "Interesting pub, the Spinners Arms. It's been here almost as long as the mill."

They went inside. The place made Rachel shudder. Elwyn was right, it was stuck way back in another era. The main bar was small, its dark brown paintwork making it look dingy. The yellowing net curtains at the windows cut out the light, filling the room with shadows. Three men stood propping up the bar, and a couple — a lad and a girl — sat at a window table.

Elwyn approached the barman. "I'm looking for Dylan Healey."

The bartender smiled. "Who wants him?"

Elwyn flashed his badge. "If he's here, just point him out."

"Him by the window."

Rachel went up and sat down next to the girl. "Dylan Healey? I'm DCI King and this is DS Pryce. We'd like to ask you some questions."

"Police? Don't know why you want me. I've done nowt."

"That mill across the road. What were you doing in there earlier today?" Rachel asked.

Dylan's eyes darted from one to the other. "Is this about them kids? They should know better than to play in there, they could get hurt. I'm surprised the parents haven't warned them. And it's patrolled, too. Get caught by one of them Shawcross men and they'd know about it."

"Talking from experience, Dylan?" asked Elwyn.

"Shawcross employs a bunch of bloody lunatics. Smack your head in soon as look at you."

The girl sitting with Healey was getting twitchy. She avoided looking Rachel in the eye and kept nudging Healey and fiddling with her hands. Rachel wondered if she was in need of a fix.

"Did you chase the boys, Dylan?" Elwyn asked.

"No. I heard 'em, scuttling about like rats. I gave 'em a warning, that's all, then I let 'em run off."

"Why warn them?" Elwyn asked. "What were you up to? Dealing?"

Healey fixed his gaze on Elwyn. He had small, evil eyes. "Don't know what you mean, copper. Me and a mate went in there to get out of the rain, that's all. We were chatting. Nowt wrong in that."

"Was it you who rang for help?" Rachel asked.

He shook his head. "Can't take the credit for that one. It was my mate. He's got the conscience, not me."

He gave Rachel a sly smile. So, if it had been up to him, he'd have left the lads in that hole. What a scumbag. "Do you know who else uses the mill?" she asked.

"Them kids. Sometimes there's a homeless guy sleeps in there. But mostly it's just empty. Folk don't even seem to notice the place any more."

"Who were you with? Who got help for the boys?" Rachel asked. "Does your mate have a name?"

"I don't know him that well. He's just someone I see around."

He was lying, it was written all over his face, but right now Rachel couldn't prove otherwise. "We'll want to speak to you again, Dylan, so don't disappear or you'll be in trouble."

"What d'you think?" Elwyn asked, once they were outside.

"No morals, and he's so used to lying he doesn't even realise he's doing it. He'll have been dealing, alright, but I don't see him as the main man, not sharp enough. Get uniform to do regular checks on that mill from now on. If they catch Healey with drugs on him, they bring him in. We could do with having a word with the security firm. They may be able to throw some light on who our victim was."

They went back to the car. "You'll have to make a decision soon," Elwyn said. "Make plans for when the baby comes."

She sighed. He was back on the subject of her pregnancy.

"You must be twelve weeks gone. You can't go much longer pretending it's not happening."

"You're stating the obvious, Elwyn. When I've decided, you'll be one of the first to know," she said sarcastically.

"And Jed?"

Jed McAteer, the baby's father and the man who'd been hovering in the shadows of her world for most of her life. That's where Rachel would have liked him to stay. But a brief liaison at a wedding in Malaga earlier in the year had got her into this mess. The truth was, whenever she was around Jed, common sense went out of the window. "I'm not sure. Tell him, and it's like offering an open door. He'll want in to my life on all levels, and I'm not ready for that yet. That's why I want to wait. I've a lot to consider. What I decide will affect the rest of my life."

Heavy stuff. Elwyn quickly changed the subject. "I'm moving into my new house on Friday. I intend to have a bit of a bash. Want to come?"

"Not this Friday, surely? Won't you want to get the place straight first?"

He grinned. "Thought you guys might help me with that. Ffion's making food, it'll be good."

"Have your parents seen the house?"

"Not yet. They're coming over from Rhos on Sunday. I hope to have it straight by then. What d'you say? A bit of down time will do you good."

"I'll see, and that's all I can promise at the mo."

"Fair enough. Right, where to now?" he asked.

"Back to the station, but first we'll give Jude a quick visit, see if she's got anything for us yet."

CHAPTER FOUR

"We've had a bit of luck," Jude said with a smile. "As expected, the newspaper the victim was lying on had disintegrated but we have found a date." she said. "Provided, of course, that whoever put them there didn't use papers they'd had for months."

Rachel's eyes were drawn to what was left of the body lying on the table. It gave rise to so many questions. What had been done to him before his death? An involuntary shudder snaked down her spine. The sight was the stuff of nightmares. "When was it?" she asked.

"The latest date we have on the newspapers is two years ten months ago."

Rachel shook her head. That was a long time. The trail would have gone cold. "Missing persons isn't much use to us without a name. Anything in his clothing?"

Jude nodded. "Most of it is in tatters but the leather jacket is in good shape and pretty distinctive. It needs work to enhance, but I think the design on the back is a name or initials that have been appliqued on." She smiled. "And this'll cheer you up. In the inside pocket, we found a debit card."

Rachel could scarcely believe their luck.

"Is it still readable? Do we have a name?" Elwyn asked.

"Well, the date and account number aren't clear at all but the name on the card is Rita Pearce. The bank will have her details."

"So the victim is a woman? You said the body was male," Rachel said.

"Rita might be the victim's girlfriend, or a family member," Jude suggested. "You won't know until you speak to her."

"Thanks, Jude." Rachel nodded at the body. "What next for him?"

"We'll clean him up and hope we can discover how he died. But he has a lot of broken bones, particularly his legs, and some are missing entirely. No doubt Jason will find them in that cellar. That can't have happened by accident or natural decomposition. I think he was beaten badly before he died."

More horror to contemplate. "If you get anything else, let me know at once," Rachel said.

"Butterfield and I will take a thorough look at the remains tomorrow. If you want to attend, I'll text you the time. But it won't be pleasant."

Not something to look forward to, but Rachel would be there. Butterfield might turn up something important and she needed to know at once. She and Elwyn made for the car.

"I want the bastard catching, Elwyn. Whoever snuffed the life out of that poor man like that thinks he's got away with it. The trail is cold but that won't stop us. I'm determined the team won't give up until we've exhausted every avenue." Her voice quivered with emotion.

"We see a lot of awful things, Rachel, but this appears to have affected you more than most," Elwyn said.

He was right, and she was embarrassed that he'd noticed. Not that Rachel was in any way hardened to what she faced in the course of her job, but she did try to present a certain detachment. "I don't know why, but please don't blame it on my condition. I am more emotional, I admit, but pregnant or not, crimes like that hit me hard. For all we know he could have been left in there to die, injured, in a confined space and unable to help himself. It doesn't bear too much thinking about."

Elwyn put an arm around her shoulder. "Chin up, Rachel. We'll all do everything in our power to get the bastard." He hugged her close to comfort her, and then let go. "He might have been dead already when they left him there," he suggested.

"No, he wasn't," Rachel said firmly. "Or whoever did it wouldn't have bothered tying him up. At least we have a name — with luck this Rita Pearce will have known our victim. We'll go back to the station, get her details and then speak to her."

* * *

Rachel assembled the team in the meeting room. The two detective constables, Jonny Farrell, and Amy Metcalf, Stella, their civilian information officer and the two uniformed PCs assigned to them.

Jonny was keen, a young, ambitious detective who worked hard. He could have had a much easier time of things if he'd chosen to go into the family business — his father, a former professional footballer, owned a string of sportswear shops across Manchester. But Jonny had always had a burning ambition to be a detective, a sentiment Rachel understood well. The other DC was not so easy to understand. What motivated her? Amy's input came in fits and starts. Sometimes she was an excellent officer, but at others she was sloppy and disinterested. Amy was also convinced that Rachel didn't like her, which was untrue, though Rachel had no time for shirkers on her team and couldn't understand why a young person would be doing the job in the first place if her heart wasn't one hundred per cent in it.

"We have the body of an unknown male, injured, and possibly left to rot in a tunnel under the dilapidated remains of Shawcross Mill for approximately three years," Rachel said.

"Murdered?" Amy asked.

"The way he was left, I would say so. We await the PM tomorrow for further details of how he died."

"Do we have anything to work with?" asked Jonny.

"We do." Rachel smiled. "Our victim was wearing a leather jacket with a debit card in the pocket. The card wasn't his. The name on that card is Rita Pearce." She looked at Jonny. "I want her finding quickly. She most likely knows who our victim is. Our first task is to give him a name and find his family. They need to be told." She turned to Amy. "Check missing persons too. It's a long shot, but let's see how many male mispers we had around that time."

"I'll get on to the bank right away, ma'am," Jonny said. "The last time that card was used might help with the timescale."

Rachel nodded. "Do that, would you? Jude has put all the forensic details gleaned so far on the system. You'll get what you need from there."

A voice spoke from the back of the room. "DCI King, when you've finished briefing the team, could I have a word? I'll wait for you in Harding's old office."

Surprised, Rachel recognised that voice only too well. It was DCI Mark Kenton. But what was he doing here? For a brief spell he'd been their acting superintendent. Prior to that, he'd been the SIO on a people trafficking case that had overlapped with a murder Rachel was working on. Relations between the pair had been strained. Rachel was aware that he'd returned to his own station at Salford, and she and the team thought they'd seen the last of him. His unexpected return filled her with trepidation. Kenton was an irritant she could do without.

CHAPTER FIVE

Kenton was waiting for her in Superintendent Harding's office, seated in the ex-super's chair. He smiled at her. "Take a seat."

Rachel was curious but she didn't have time for polite conversation. "What's going on, Mark?" she asked. "Why are you back?"

"Coffee?" he said, ignoring her question.

"No thanks. Just tell me what you're doing here."

"Well, Harding doesn't need this office any more. He lost his job, if you remember."

Rachel's eyes darted around the small room. She saw Kenton's overcoat on a hanger behind the door and the contents of his briefcase spread over the desk. She groaned — she couldn't help it. "You've got Harding's job, haven't you? You're our new super."

He smiled. "You should be a detective! Well done, spot on. Apparently, I did such a good job as *acting* super the powers that be thought they'd make it permanent." He paused, watching her closely. "I have to say, Rachel, I was surprised you didn't offer up any competition for the post. A career-minded woman like you — it was the logical next step."

If only. And he was right, in other circumstances, Rachel would have been a strong contender. But she was pregnant and no matter what provisions the force had for mothers with infants, it would just not have worked. When she'd had her other two children, she'd had Alan, their father. This time she'd be on her own.

"I have my reasons."

He looked puzzled. "Care to share them? Is there something I should know about the role? Or the station?"

"No, Mark, the teams here are excellent, particularly mine, and everyone is very friendly. But a word of advice, don't be too hard to start with and ruffle too many feathers. You need their support."

"I'll do my best. I'm a fair man, but I am used to getting results."

Rachel knew that. She also knew that his team at Salford had been scared stiff of him. Kenton had a temper, and if things didn't go as he expected, he wasn't afraid to show it. If he threw his weight around here, the positive dynamic within her team would suffer.

"Now, your current case. I'd have thought it would've been more suited to the cold case team."

Rachel wasn't about to take that from him. "You're wrong. The body is on our patch and we'll cope just fine."

"Mistake, Rachel. The forensic costs alone will run to a small fortune. We have a tight budget. I'll give you a week to make progress. After that, cold case has it."

So, this was how it was going to be. Everything they did, he'd lay down the law, standing over her team with a bloody calculator in his hand. Well, she wasn't having it.

"We've already got a strong lead, Mark. Leave us to it." Rachel had heard enough. She stood up to leave.

"I mean it, Rachel. You have one week. The budget isn't infinite, and I will not throw it at cases we should pass on elsewhere."

"We can't solve crimes, particularly a murder as nasty as this one, on a shoestring, Mark. We're detectives, not accountants." She turned her back on him and headed for the door.

"Seen Jed recently?" he called after he.

Rachel stopped in her tracks. Was it the name or the fact that Kenton had asked the question? Rachel wasn't sure. Jed was a problem she couldn't think about rationally just now. She had no idea what she was going to do about him or the baby, when or even if she was going to tell him. And discussing their relationship with Kenton was not on the menu.

"No, why?"

"We had lunch a couple of days ago. He thinks you're avoiding him. Is that the case?"

"Whether I avoid Jed McAteer or not has nothing to do with you," she said.

Rachel was dying to ask Kenton what he was doing having lunch with Jed in the first place, but she bit her tongue. The two men were poles apart. Kenton was a career cop, while back in the day, Jed had been one of Manchester's most notorious villains — which was why he and Rachel weren't together. However, of late, Jed had magically swept all that away and the police, Kenton in particular, appeared to think Jed had changed.

"Jed is concerned that he's heard nothing from you these last weeks. He blames me for working you too hard. I assured him that wasn't so."

"Work keeps us all busy, Mark." She'd no idea what his game was. Why all the interest in her relationship — or otherwise — with Jed? "Jed understands that."

"Are you sure? He struck me as one puzzled man. He spoke about you constantly, told me how the pair of you met as students. He never married, so I presume he must have been carrying a torch for you all these years."

That was no business of his. Rachel wanted to give him a piece of her mind, but she held her tongue. What was Jed doing discussing their private life with this man? Kenton must have read the look on her face because all at once he changed tack.

"Okay, I'll drop it. Keep me informed about the case, and remember, you have a week."

Rachel was shaking when she left Kenton's office. At this rate she'd fall apart within days. She had to get a grip. Whether it was the case, Jed or the pregnancy, she'd no idea. But it had to stop. She had a job to do, with or without Kenton on her back. She decided to keep Kenton's ultimatum to herself. The team wouldn't take it well, and she needed all their concentration on the case, not fretting about deadlines.

CHAPTER SIX

Back in the incident room, Elwyn had put up photos on the board showing the narrow tunnel where the body was found, and the interior of the mill. The images of the victim and how he'd been left made Rachel shudder. The sooner they caught the killer, the better.

"Amy, will you check the system for any similar killings? Anything that correlates to what we've got here," Rachel said.

"We've had a hit on the bank card," Jonny said. "Rita Pearce works at the Spinners Arms on Shawcross Street. She reported it stolen nearly three years ago and had it cancelled."

"The timescale fits and that pub is across from the mill," Rachel noted. "In fact, me and Elwyn were in there earlier." She caught the Welshman's eye. "Time to go back, I think, have a proper word with the staff." She looked at Jonny. "Do we have the date she cancelled it?"

"Yes, it's the same week as the one on the newspaper Jude has."

"Do we know when we can have a closer look at the area where the body was found?" she asked Elwyn.

"It's a health and safety problem apparently. Until they've given the all-clear, no one can get close, not even forensics."

Amy was sifting through a list on a printout. "I'm trying to find out exactly who rented those units," she said. "I'm waiting for the Shawcross Estate office to ring me back with more information.

"When they do, tell them we'll be needing a word. Find out who we need to speak to. We'll get the estate's take on this, find out why they shut the units and have allowed the mill to rot. In fact, anyone who had anything to do with that mill in the last three years must be interviewed. Help her with the research, Jonny, and stay on it until you get what we need."

She had to say something about Kenton. They'd all seen him earlier and were no doubt curious. Telling them he was their new boss would not go down well.

"We have a permanent replacement for Harding," she announced. "Mark Kenton." She paused for a moment to let the news sink in. Their faces said it all. She was right, they weren't happy. "He'll be more hands-on than Harding. Until we get the measure of exactly how things will change, we'll just have to watch our step."

"You should have gone for it, ma'am," Jonny said. "You'd have been great. I think you made a big mistake there, if you don't mind me saying."

She tried to shrug it off, but he was right. The post had come up just when she was least able to go for it. "Well it's too late now, Jonny. And please believe me when I say I have my own reasons for leaving the job well alone." She knew there was bound to be a debate about that once she left the office.

* * *

"Kenton's been lunching with Jed," Rachel told Elwyn. "What do you imagine that pair had to talk about?"

"You," he said without hesitation.

"Perhaps, but unlikely as it may seem, I think that the two of them are friends and have known each other for a

26

while. They collaborated, remember, during the Rafferty case. Jed went along with being labelled as the bad guy and scarpered off to Spain."

Daniel Rafferty was the man behind the people trafficking Kenton had been investigating when his and Rachel's paths had first crossed. Kenton and Jed had lulled the villain into a false sense of security by making it appear that Jed was the prime suspect in the case. That allowed Rafferty to take stock and resume his business, secure in the belief that the police hadn't a clue about what was really going on. The ruse had worked, and now Rafferty was safely behind bars. That was as it should be, but what bothered Rachel was the friendship that had developed between Jed and her new boss.

With Elwyn behind the wheel, the two detectives made their way to the Spinners Arms on Shawcross Street. Rachel was distracted, her thoughts anywhere but on the case. Elwyn Pryce had known her long enough to guess her state of mind.

"You need to sort it," he said, "and as soon as possible. You tell Jed about the baby and you arrange your maternity leave with Kenton."

Kenton! Rachel could well imagine what he'd make of it. She could see the smirk on his face and hear the sarcasm in his voice as he quizzed her about Jed.

"Leave it, Elwyn. I'll sort things in my own time."

"Well, get it done pronto, that's my advice."

Rachel didn't like Elwyn's tone. It had an edge to it, which was unusual for him. "I'll leave things until I've at least had a scan, if you don't mind," she said. "It's all still uncertain, anything might happen. You may have forgotten but I've got a big birthday later this year. I'll be forty years old by the time I give birth. Mother nature, in her wisdom, meant for women to reproduce long before they reach that age. I could well be going to the antenatal clinic with women half my age. And I don't like being told what to do, even by you, Elwyn."

"You're worried, that's what it is, isn't it?" he said. "Plenty of women in their forties have babies. You've no need to be anxious, Rachel. But it makes no sense to struggle on pretending it isn't happening. You can't take for ever to think it out."

Elwyn had no idea. To him, it was a simple matter. But the reality was that having a baby would change her life. Plus, telling her daughters and ex-husband about it could well shatter their world.

"Jed and Kenton I can handle, it's telling Alan and the kids that's scaring the hell out of me," she admitted. "How's Alan going to react? The poor man's done nothing but support me and the kids. Even though we're divorced, he works from home so he can be there for the girls. He never complains, he shops, cooks and sorts stuff out so that things at home go smoothly even when I'm not there. He'll want to know everything, and then the kids will ask questions. Who can blame them? I'd be the same. As far as they're concerned, I don't have a man in my life. I daren't mention Jed. Mia is already suspicious about him. She asked me outright if he was her real dad."

"I didn't say it'd be easy, but you can't keep it secret. Give it a few weeks and they'll see for themselves that you're pregnant, and then they'll want to know why you didn't tell them."

They were pulling on to Shawcross Street, so they'd have to put an end to the conversation for now. Nevertheless, Elwyn wanted to get his point across. "You might consider telling Mia the truth, you know. You'd save yourself a lot of stress if it was all out in the open."

"You think so?" she retorted. "Sometimes, Elwyn, you just don't get it."

CHAPTER SEVEN

Rita Pearce kept herself to herself. She'd lived in the area a long time, knew everyone and most of what went on but had learned the hard way that silence was the best bet. To those who spoke to her in passing, Rita might appear reserved or even shy, but that wasn't it. Rita was married to a brute of a man and daren't say a word out of place, fearing for her own safety and that of her daughter, Jasmine. Not that Jaz couldn't stick up for herself. She was feisty and gave as good as she got. The problem was, Ray had no qualms about lashing out at either of them.

As landlady of the Spinners Arms, she heard a lot of gossip. While she worked behind the bar, people told her things, but she made it a rule not to pass comment. "A good listener," folk called her, and that was fine by Rita. No one knew the truth of what she endured except Kath Madison, one of the barmaids and her friend. She'd seen the bruises on Rita's face, and the attempts to cover her husband's handiwork with make-up. Kath asked questions but got little in return. Until the night Ray broke Ruth's arm, that was, and Kath took her to A & E. Kath tried to persuade her friend to leave the animal. But Rita refused, made excuses, said he'd promised to change. But he never did.

* * *

When Rachel and Elwyn arrived, Rita was on duty behind the bar. Around fifty, she was tall, her short dark hair not yet greying. She eyed the two strangers warily. Rachel had seen that look before and had often wondered how people sensed who they were before they had spoken a single word.

"We're looking for Rita Pearce, the landlady," Rachel said.

Rita smiled tentatively. "That's me."

"DCI King and DS Pryce from East Manchester CID." Rachel reached into her pocket for her mobile and showed Rita an image of the leather jacket and bank card. "The bank card is yours. Can you tell us how it came to be in the pocket of this jacket?"

Rita Pearce stared at the images, and her mouth fell open. "Where did you find it after all this time? I thought that was gone for ever."

"How did it go missing?" Rachel asked. She watched the woman's eyes dart about the room. She was tense about something. When she realised the pub was empty except for the three of them, she seemed to relax slightly.

She pointed to the hallway. "If I'd been shopping, I used to hang my bag and coat on a hook behind the door there. The bag was hidden from view but the debit card was inside. I always presumed it was stolen one night when I was working. I didn't notice it was gone until I was at the supermarket on the Friday afternoon. I searched everywhere, thinking I'd lost it. But when other things went missing, stuff belonging to customers, I finally had to admit the truth. We had a thief. But I couldn't think of anyone who'd want to steal from me. I cancelled the card the day after I discovered it was gone. I was lucky, it hadn't been used."

Elwyn showed her the image of the jacket. "Do you know who might have owned this? It's got lettering on the back. Our forensics people will clean it up, but you might have seen it before."

Rita shook her head. "Sorry, no. It might have belonged to a customer, but I don't recognise it."

"We were told that at one time there were a number of units on the ground floor of the mill over there. There was a man working with leather I believe," Elwyn said. "Could it one of his?"

Rita nodded. "It could be. The jacket looks like a one-off, which was his speciality."

"Do you recall his name?" Rachel asked.

"No. All sorts of craftspeople rented space over there. The place was booming at one time. But they didn't last long, a few months, and then they all had to leave."

"Why was that?" asked Rachel.

"Shawcross," Rita said. "One day his manager turned up and gave them all notice, told them in no uncertain terms to clear off. The place has been empty ever since."

A teenage girl came up to the bar and stood beside Rita. "You okay, Mum?" she asked, scowling at Rachel.

"Fine, love. These are police officers. They found my bank card. Remember, it went missing?" She turned to Rachel and Elwyn. "This is my daughter, Jasmine."

"Tell us about the night your card was stolen," Elwyn said.

"I'm not really sure. It could have been any time that week, and it was three years ago anyway. We get all sorts in here, it could have been anyone."

"Do you have any suspicions about who might have taken it?"

"No. Back then, with the mill being so busy, we were packed every night. Not like these days." She gave them a quizzical look. "Why the interest now? I reported it at the time but back then you lot didn't want to know."

The girl folded her arms and glared at them. "Yeah, go on. Why now?"

"I expect you'll have heard about the body found in the mill?" Elwyn said. Rita nodded. "Your debit card was found on him."

Rita Pearce turned pale. "You think the victim stole my card?"

"Do you know who he is?" Rachel asked.

"No. How could I? Whatever went on over there had nothing to do with me."

"We're not accusing you of anything, Rita," Rachel said gently. "You live and work around here, people use this pub, you'd notice if someone suddenly stopped coming in. Do you recall anyone like that?"

"Not off the top of my head. How long had the body been there?"

"Roughly three years," Elwyn said.

"Like I said, we were busy. Plenty of folk visited the mill and those units. The bloke who fixed cars was open seven days until late. The poor sod you found could be anyone, and not necessarily someone from round here."

Enough questions for now. Rita Pearce was becoming agitated. Rachel handed her a card. "If anything occurs to you, Rita, give us a ring."

Back outside, the detectives looked up and down the road. A group of reporters were hanging about at the entrance to the mill.

"What d'you think?" Elwyn asked.

"What, of that bunch? Not a lot."

"Not them. Rita Pearce. I thought she was twitchy. She gave me the impression she was holding something back."

Rachel shrugged. "Perhaps."

"What now?"

"It's gone six, so I'm off home. I'll drop you at the station."

"Have that chat with Alan tonight," Elwyn suggested. "It'll clear the air and you'll feel tons better."

Good advice, but it could just as easily backfire. Her ex-husband would not take the news well. Rachel decided she'd give it some consideration.

* * *

The minute the detectives were out of the building, Rita Pearce helped herself to a brandy. She was shaking badly.

Kath Madison appeared from the back room and put a hand on her shoulder. "No need to tell me, I can guess. They were police, right?"

Rita nodded. She turned around and glanced into the corridor that led to their flat. She needed to make sure Jaz had left. "That body from the mill. They found my missing debit card with it."

"It was stolen, everyone knows that. Perhaps some homeless bloke took it."

Rita shook her head. "You don't believe that any more than I do." She took a slug of the brandy. "I think that body is Gav's. And if it is, you know what that means."

"Look, that brute you're married to is a lot of things, but he isn't a killer. He hits you because you don't fight back. Gav was a big bloke, well able to take care of himself. If Ray tried anything, he'd have made mincemeat of him."

But Rita wasn't convinced. That body was Gav's, she just knew it.

CHAPTER EIGHT

The A6 was busy and traffic slow, so Rachel had plenty of time to think on her way home. Elwyn was right, this wouldn't keep. When it came down to it, she was more afraid of telling Mia, her youngest daughter, than anyone else. Mia'd know at once who the father of the unborn child was, and it would confirm her suspicions that Jed was her father too. Well, that particular uncomfortable truth must stay secret for now. Mia was only fourteen and wouldn't understand. Apart from which, it would devastate Alan.

Darkness had fallen. The lane where Rachel lived was usually still and quiet but tonight her house was noisy, lights blazing out into the night sky. The house sat on a country lane in the Cheshire village of Poynton, and there were no nosey neighbours to peer in through the open curtains or hear the loud music and raucous laughter. Rachel had no idea what was going on, just that it appeared to be some sort of celebration.

An excited Alan met her in the hallway and gave her a peck on the cheek. "Rachel! Come through. We've got champagne on the go."

What was the champagne for? "No, I couldn't. I need to eat something first. I've hardly managed a bite all day. After that I could do with a word."

Alan, her ex-husband, lived in the semi-detached cottage adjoining Rachel's. It was an unusual set-up for a divorced couple, but the arrangement suited them. Their two daughters had the run of both houses and divided their time between them. For their sakes, Rachel and Alan had remained friends, so it worked out well.

He was smiling broadly. "Belinda's here. We've got something to tell you."

Belinda Bellamy and Alan had been an item for a while. She was a little older than Alan and ran a small local farm and shop, mostly on her own, which she complained about all the time.

"Is this what I think it is?" Rachel asked, scrutinising that smile. "Are you moving in with her?"

Before Alan could reply, Mia rushed up to greet her mother.

"Isn't it great? Me and Megan will be bridesmaids."

Rachel stared at Alan, who was nodding vigorously. "That's right. Me and Belinda are getting married."

"Married!" Rachel echoed. "Isn't it all, well, a bit soon?"

"No, it's just perfect. I love Belinda and she loves me." He put a reassuring arm around Rachel's shoulder. "It won't change anything between us four. The girls will still be at the centre of my life and I will always look out for you."

Rachel smiled. That wasn't true. This and the baby would change everything. Life in the King household would never be the same again. "I wish you luck. You deserve to be happy, Alan. Will Belinda move in with you?"

"That's another big change," he said. "I'm selling the house."

This really threw her off balance. Rachel was silent for a moment, stunned. Of course, she had no right to dictate where Alan lived, but having him next door had been a god-send while the girls were growing up.

"You're moving in with her?"

"No, we want a fresh start, so Belinda is selling the farm. She's keeping the shop — it's doing well and gives her a reasonable income. We're buying a property together. We've seen something we like in Bollington."

Bollington was on the outskirts of Macclesfield. It wasn't far. "You'll have to take me to see it," she said.

"I will. Come on through. I've made food. I'll get you something."

Her daughters, Megan and Mia, were in the kitchen chatting to Belinda. Belinda was a big woman but strong, not flabby. She came forward and almost crushed skinny Rachel in an enormous hug.

"You're not upset about this, are you? I know you and Alan are still close."

Rachel shook her head. "We're friends, that's all," She smiled. "I'm very happy for you both. A new house, too. Are you okay with that? That farm has been your life."

"And my father's before me. It's time to let it go, Rachel. I've slogged away at it for far too long. It's damned hard work and I hate the early mornings. The shop will do me fine. I'll get stock from all the farms in the area and the family who are buying my farm will continue to supply me."

"Wonder who I'll get next door?" mused Rachel.

"He's told the estate agent in the village. There have been a number of enquiries already, I believe," Belinda said.

Whoever bought Alan's cottage would have to be pretty easy-going. With two teenage daughters, at times the noise was off the scale. And soon there would be a baby to add to the mix.

"What was it you wanted to tell me?" Alan asked. "Important, is it?"

Rachel shook her head. "It's nothing that won't wait."

CHAPTER NINE

Wednesday

As Rachel arrived at work the following morning she was greeted by an excited Jonny. "I've got an appointment with the manager from Shawcross Estates this morning, ma'am," he said. "He didn't sound happy about talking to us, or having a body found on the premises. Apparently, the mill is about to be put up for sale. He's worried it'll put prospective buyers off."

"Why now, I wonder? It's stood empty for years and all of a sudden, it's on the market." Rachel went to her office, curious about this development. She poured herself an orange juice and toyed with the idea of asking Jed. He was a developer and knew the property market in Manchester like the back of his hand. He was bound to know what was going on. But it would be tantamount to inviting him back into her life, and she wasn't ready for that yet.

"Jonny!" she shouted. "I'll come with you to see the bloke from Shawcross." She'd have to speak to them about the tenants anyway.

Elwyn stuck his head around her office door. "Dylan Healey is in the cells," he said. "He was back in the mill last night, smoking weed, and was stopped by one of the uniforms. He kicked up a right fuss, which ended with him assaulting PC Holt, hence his arrest. Want to speak to him?"

"You do it, Elwyn. I'm off to see the manager of Shawcross Estates. It'll do no harm to get a feel of what they're like."

"Orange juice?"

"Not my usual morning tipple, I know, but strong coffee is out the window at the moment."

"Are you okay?" he asked.

"Not really," she said. "A lot to think about, both personal and workwise. We have to move on this one, Elwyn. Not a word to the others — I don't want them rattled — but Kenton has given me a week to wrap the case up."

"And if we don't?"

"Cold cases get it. He's not been in the job two minutes, and he's penny-pinching already."

"Never mind the case, are *you* okay?"

"I know what you meant." She smiled. Elwyn had that concerned expression on his face, the one she recognised only too well. What to tell him? She wasn't ready to discuss the Alan thing with anyone just yet, not even Elwyn. "Relax, Elwyn, all's fine."

* * *

Shawcross Hall occupied a prime position above the village of Prestbury, not far from Macclesfield. The house had been built by the first mill owner, Thomas Shawcross, and the family had run the business from there ever since.

As the house appeared at the end of the long, winding driveway, Jonny's eyes widened. "It's huge. More like a stately home than a family house. What d'you reckon he's like?"

"I've never met any of them, so I couldn't say. Back in the day, the Shawcross family were like royalty, particularly in Ancoats — not that they ever lived there. They employed most of the population around the mill and owned all the houses the workers lived in."

"Wonder what he's like, the main man?"

"I doubt he's as grand as his ancestor. Thomas Shawcross must have really thought he was something to build a pile like this. Mathew is forty-seven and I would imagine he has to work hard for every penny like the rest of us. Cotton isn't king any more, Jonny. That mill is rotting away, and I presume there's no money to stop it doing so."

"You've done your research, ma'am."

"A quick internet search last night, that's all."

"I did some research too," Jonny said. "He has some investments that must bring in a reasonable income, but I found nothing that would keep this little lot going."

"Perhaps he's living off family money," Rachel said. "They made a small fortune out of that mill well into the twentieth century."

"Don't forget there were a number of court cases," Jonny said. "Cotton lung was a killer. One successful claim back in the seventies opened the floodgates. I don't know what's left, but I'll lay odds the firm's funds were seriously depleted."

They parked up by the main entrance, and saw a man approach from the rear of the car. Smiling, he tapped on the passenger window.

"Come on inside, I'll organise some tea."

Rachel wound down the window and showed him her warrant card. "We've got an appointment with the estate manager."

"I know, but Andrew is busy with a domestic matter. You'll have to make do with me, I'm afraid."

"And you are?" Jonny asked.

"Mathew Shawcross." He grinned. "There's nothing about this place or the mill that I don't know."

So, this was the man himself. He wasn't at all what Rachel had been expecting. He was a lot friendlier, for one, not at all put out by a visit from the police.

They followed him inside. The huge square hall was magnificent. A crystal chandelier hung from the ceiling, with matching lights adorning the walls. The walls themselves were covered in an elaborate patterned wallpaper and adorned with family portraits. Against one wall stood a large antique cabinet, filled with porcelain figures. The whole place reminded Rachel of a museum exhibition.

"Those are my bloody ancestors," Shawcross explained. "I'd shift the lot of them if I could, but he —" he pointed to one, "that's the man himself, Thomas — stipulated in his will that the place was to stay just as he'd left it. Which is a bit of a bugger, to be honest. There's nothing comfortable about nineteenth-century furniture."

He took them into a large dining room and then through that to a much smaller sitting room with a conservatory attached.

"We tend to live in the rooms on this side of the house. The place might look impressive but it's far too large to use all of it, and it's cold, even in the summer."

Rachel looked around. This room was modern with two large sofas and a large flat-screen TV on the wall. Tidy enough, except for a pile of cardboard boxes stacked in a corner.

"Those belong to my daughter, Millie," he explained. "She's about to move out. Millie and a friend have got themselves a place in town. Can't say I'm thrilled, I'll miss her, but what d'you do? You can't keep them for ever and she's old enough to please herself."

Rachel knew from her research that Mathew Shawcross was a divorcee and had only the one daughter. He would be lonely, rattling round in this huge pile on his own.

"You do know about the body that was found in the mill?" Jonny asked.

Shawcross gestured for them to sit down. "Yes, of course, dreadful business. I did hope it was nothing untoward. A homeless person, perhaps, who'd fallen foul of the weather. That would have been bad enough, but it was murder, I'm told."

"Yes, it was," Rachel said. "We urgently need to find out who he was and then contact his family."

"Anything I can do to help, just ask," Shawcross said.

"A list of all your tenants going back three years will do for starters," Jonny said. He passed Shawcross an image of the leather jacket. "There's this, too. Do you happen to know who it might belong to?"

Shawcross took a good look and shook his head. "I should have said, I haven't actually set foot in the mill for years. In the days when we let the units, my manager collected the rents."

"We'll need his details too," Jonny said.

"Yes, of course. He still works for me. Back then there were others too, but they have left."

A young woman entered the room and put a suitcase down beside the boxes.

"This is Millie, my daughter," Shawcross said. "These are police officers," he told her. "They're here about the body found in the mill."

Millie Shawcross was staring at Jonny. "Jonno?" she said. "It is you, isn't it?" Her face broke into a smile. "It's been ages, but you've hardly changed at all."

Jonny Farrell looked embarrassed. "Millie and I knew each other at university, ma'am."

Millie was attractive, tall with blonde hair. She looked very like her father.

"Police? I was convinced you'd join your father's empire, Jonno. What happened? Wouldn't he have you?"

Jonny shrugged. "I didn't fancy it, and anyway I always wanted to be a detective."

She pulled a face. "But the things you do, the sights you see — the murder in our mill being a case in point. That building should have been pulled down years ago. If it had, perhaps that poor bloke would still be alive." She looked at her father. "I don't know why you insist on keeping it. It's obviously a death trap. Some poor sod was killed there, surely you have to do something now?" She turned to Jonny. "I've got to get on, this lot wants putting in my car."

Jonny picked up one of the boxes. "I'll give you a hand."

"Millie doesn't understand," Shawcross said as the two of them left the room. "How can I pull the place down? It made this family's fortune and provided a living for most of Ancoats in its day. Thomas would turn in his grave if it was destroyed."

"But it is dangerous, Mr Shawcross," Rachel said. "It's crumbling away, and the roof is unsafe. The local kids keep breaking in, and at least one young man is using it as a venue to deal drugs. They have been warned but that won't stop them. There could be a nasty incident anytime. Health and Safety have looked around and they're not happy."

His face fell. "I know. They've been on the phone. Whether I like it or not, Shawcross Mill is coming to the end of its days. I'll just have to face facts. I've had my head in the sand for years, but it's a terrible decision to make. I'll be tearing down my family's history."

"A difficult decision," Rachel said. "But it's a brown-field site within hailing distance of the city. I'm surprised the developers haven't been falling over themselves to take it off your hands."

He smiled. "Well, if they are, they haven't spoken to me."

"And your security firm — the locals are running rings around them," she said. "Given the dealing and now the discovery of that body, it needs tightening up."

"The firm I use only does the rounds every twelve hours. They patrol the perimeter and the ground floor."

"The locals have their routine sussed, as do the kids who play in there," Rachel said.

"I'll get on to them, increase the watch," Shawcross said. "I'd hate it if anyone else got hurt. One is bad enough."

Rachel stood up. "If you give me those details, we'll be on our way."

"Yes of course. Give me a moment." He got to his feet and disappeared. Minutes later, he returned with a printout. "Here you are. Everyone who's had anything to do with the mill during the last three years. It's all there, the security firm and the details of my employees."

Rachel smiled. "Thanks. You've been very helpful."

"I'll see you out."

They walked back through the opulent hallway to the front door. "Have you ever thought of opening this place to the public?" asked Rachel.

"Heavens, no. Him up there would never forgive me." He nodded up at Thomas's portrait. "Although I have to say, the money would come in handy."

"Hard times?"

Rachel hadn't meant her remark to be taken seriously. Her tone had been flippant, but the expression on Shawcross's smile changed to a grimace.

"Very much so. The family fortunes are not what they were."

* * *

"It's good to see you again, Millie," Jonny told the girl. "I'm surprised you're leaving this place, it's a fabulous house."

"It's a prison, Jonno, believe me. I'll never have any freedom while I'm living with my father. He's so controlling. You should ask my mother."

"I had no idea. Is he the way he is because your mother left?"

"My mother left because of the way he is. He made her life a misery, but she got out eventually and made another life for herself. She even got engaged." Millie smiled. "You should have seen him trying to get his head round that one. He's one jealous man at times."

"Jonny!" Rachel called to him. "Time to go."

Jonny pecked Millie on the cheek. "Take care."

Back in the car, Rachel asked Jonny what he thought.

"Millie's scared of him — her own father. She's leaving because of his jealousy and his controlling nature."

"That's not the impression I got. I thought he was nice, open and friendly."

"Involved in the case?"

"I wouldn't think so, Jonny. He's too wrapped up with this place and keeping it afloat. The mill is probably a huge inconvenience, and one that's going to cost him money he hasn't got, from all accounts." As far as she was concerned, Mathew Shawcross had been candid with them. "Now, what is it with you and his daughter, Millie? You said nothing about knowing the family."

"I don't, ma'am, not much, anyway. I was surprised to see her here. When we were at university, she called herself Millie Fenwick. I never associated her with the Shawcross family."

Rachel thought for a moment. "Do you know what happened to Millie's mother?"

"She left him and took up with another man. I've no idea who, but it caused quite a stir at the time. Vanessa Shawcross left here with Millie in tow. I presume that's when Millie took to using her mother's name of Fenwick."

"But she does call herself Shawcross these days. She's on the electoral register. Make that call and arrange to meet. See if you can find out more about the divorce."

"Is it important, ma'am?"

"Well, it's background and you never know."

"And, ma'am . . . please don't tell the team about her calling me Jonno. I couldn't stand the teasing."

Grinning, Rachel nudged his arm. "It'll cost you, Detective Constable."

CHAPTER TEN

Elwyn and Amy sat in the interview room facing Dylan Healey and the duty solicitor. Healey did not appear to be in the least bothered by his arrest. He gave the two detectives a friendly nod before stretching out his long legs and sitting back, relaxed.

His attitude niggled Elwyn. Petty villains like Healey saw nothing wrong in their antics. "You've had numerous warnings but yet again, you've been caught in Shawcross Mill, using," Elwyn said.

Healey shrugged. "A bit of weed, that's all, nothing heavy."

Not the slightest hint of remorse. "It's still against the law, Dylan," Amy warned. "And this isn't the first time. Were you dealing too?"

"Look, I hold my hands up to using, and hitting that copper, but I'm small fry. You're missing a trick, pissing around with me when you should be sorting out the real problem." Healey had a grin on his face. "You've no idea, have you? You lot haven't the first clue about what's really going on. I'm not the problem, believe me."

That sparked Elwyn's curiosity. They'd no idea that there was serious dealing going on at the mill. "Perhaps you'd like to tell us more, Dylan," Elwyn said.

"Not my place," he said immediately. "Speak to you lot and I get my head bashed in. I've already said too much as it is."

Elwyn couldn't let this go. Was this just Healey spouting rubbish, or something else? "What are you telling us? That there's a problem with dealing at that mill, and no one's noticed?"

"Oh, folk notice, alright. They just don't tell you lot. Drugs are big business. The problem in my area is well established. It's hush-hush and it runs like clockwork."

"I don't believe you," Elwyn said. "Tell us what you mean, Dylan. We need details."

"No jobs, no prospects, families with nowt and some poor sods with a habit to feed . . . Think about it, copper. There's a lot of users out there. Like I said, big business. Someone is making a fortune but it ain't me. I'm just an occasional user who sees stuff, a shadow no one notices."

Elwyn looked at the young man trying to work out if he was telling the truth. "You're saying the dealing and drug problem is much bigger in that area than we realised?"

"Bright one, aren't you?" Dylan grinned at Elwyn. "Take a gold star."

Ignoring the sarcasm, Elwyn asked, "Exactly what are you saying, Dylan? Be more precise."

"Nowt. That's all you're getting. I've said too much as it is. I don't want to end up like him you found. But if I was you, I'd keep a watch on that mill. You never know what else you might discover."

"What are you talking about? More bodies?" asked Amy.

"I don't know, but nothing would surprise me."

* * *

"Do we attach any importance to what Healey told us?" Amy asked as they left the room.

"I'll make enquiries, see if there've been any complaints about dealing in that area. Forensics are searching the mill, so we'll wait and see what they come up with too. Make a note on the board," he said.

"The drug problem, if there is one, could be a motive," Amy said. "Get on the wrong side of a dealer and they're brutal."

"Agreed, but at the moment, it's simply conjecture. Healey is a known liar. He'd say anything to save his skin."

"Are we charging him?" she asked.

"With assault? Too right we are."

Elwyn was only too aware that time was passing, and they had neither a name for the victim, nor a motive for his murder. Was it down to a vengeful dealer as Amy thought? Or was that too simple?

Rachel had texted him a list of the tenants who'd had units in the mill. There were ten, and every one of them would have to be found and interviewed. Not an easy task.

"Stella, see what you can do with this. They all had units in Shawcross Mill at one time."

Stella was the team's information officer and admin assistant. She took the list and read through it. "I know him," she said. "Andy Siddall used to be a mechanic until his accident."

"Andy's Autos?" Elwyn asked.

"Yep, until his right hand got busted and he lost everything. Mind you, he must have done something right. Up until that time he lived in Ardwick, by the Apollo, these days he's living in a nice little bungalow in Reddish. I'll find the number."

"Thanks. We'll start with him."

CHAPTER ELEVEN

Siddall's bungalow was on a small crescent of similar properties near the golf course in Reddish.

"He lives in number five," Amy said. "There — that one."

"Do we have any information other than what Stella told us?" Elwyn said.

Amy flipped through the notes. "No. He ran his own car repair business from the mill until the accident, after which he had to give up."

"Not on our system, then?"

"No, he's never been in trouble."

"Do we know anything about his accident?"

She shrugged. "Nothing here."

Elwyn rang the bell. They heard a dog bark and several minutes later a tallish man opened the door. "Andy Siddall?"

He backed away slightly, looking them up and down. "Who wants to know?"

"We're police," Elwyn said. "CID. We're investigating a murder at Shawcross Mill. Can we come in?"

"No, it'll upset the dog. I read about that in the paper. Poor sod, whoever he was."

"That's why we're here. We've no identity for the victim. You ran your business from the mill at one time, so anything you can recall might help."

"I wasn't the only one who worked from there, there was a bunch of us. It could have been anyone."

Amy passed him the image of the leather jacket. "We will be talking to the others but in the meantime, would you take a look? We believe this belonged to the victim. Have you seen it before?"

Siddall coughed. When he raised his right hand to cover his mouth, the detectives saw the black glove.

"Bad was it, the injury?" Elwyn asked.

"Too right it was. It finished me. I was a sole trader. Business wasn't always good, and I couldn't afford fancy insurance. Know what that means?"

Elwyn nodded. "No pay-out."

"Can't you work at all?" Amy asked.

Siddall removed the glove. The hand was unrecognisable, completely mangled and with three fingers missing. "The ramp failed, my hand got caught under it, took the full force. The surgeon wanted to amputate but I refused permission. I had no choice but to lose the fingers, no circulation in them. I thought, no matter how bad, half a hand was better than none."

Amy looked at the damaged flesh. "I'm very sorry. It must have made things hard."

"It did, but I just have to get on with it."

"You haven't done too bad though." Elwyn smiled. "Since the accident you've got out of Ardwick and bought this place."

"I've worked all my life, until this." He held up his hand. "I used my savings and got a mortgage."

"The jacket?" Elwyn reminded.

He shook his head dismissively. "Sorry, no. I've no idea who owned it."

"It's quite distinctive," Amy said. "We're not sure yet, but the name on the back could be 'Gav.' Does that ring any bells?"

Siddall shook his head again. "I kept myself to myself, got on with my work. Business fluctuated but I did have my busy spells. The mill was a vibrant place back then, lots of units, people coming and going all the time. That poor man could be anyone."

Elwyn handed him a card. "If you do remember anything, give me a ring."

* * *

"Poor man, his hand is in a right state," Amy said as they went back to the car.

Elwyn ignored her comment. He had every sympathy, but Siddall had said nothing to help the case and Elwyn had the feeling it was deliberate. It was frustrating. They badly needed a break or very soon they'd have Kenton on their backs. "I got the impression that he was hiding something. Did you believe his story about the injury?"

"What are you suggesting, sir?"

"I'm not sure, but everywhere we go we hit a brick wall and that bothers me. Someone must know who our victim was, or at the very least have one or two suggestions. That jacket is fairly special. See it once and you'd remember."

While they were talking, Elwyn noticed a woman walking in their direction. It was Rita Pearce from the Spinners Arms.

Elwyn looked at her in surprise. "Mrs Pearce. What are you doing here?"

The woman looked away and lowered her head. "I don't see that it's any of your business, but if you must know, a friend of mine lives in one of these." She nodded at the bungalows.

This was too much of a coincidence. "Is that friend Andy Siddall, by any chance?"

"No!" she exclaimed. "I haven't seen Andy in ages. I'd no idea he even lived along here."

Elwyn bent down and peered more closely into her face. He thought so. The woman had a black eye, which she'd tried to conceal with make-up.

"Who gave you that?" Elwyn asked.

"It's nothing. I fell against a kitchen cupboard."

"It looks really sore."

"Look, I've got to go. I can't stand around here talking, it's cold."

"You do remember Andy, then?"

"Yes, of course I do, he fixed our car a couple of times."

"Did you know about his accident?" Elwyn asked.

She looked away. "I heard something about it. He had to give up working, I believe."

"Okay, we'll let you get on." Elwyn smiled at her and stood aside.

They watched her walk past Siddall's place until she disappeared around the corner.

"She's lying too," Elwyn said. "There seems to be some sort of conspiracy going on. No one who had anything to do with that mill will tell us the truth about what really went on there."

CHAPTER TWELVE

Rachel had only been back in her office a matter of minutes when Jude rang.

"I haven't done the full PM yet but there have been some interesting developments. Could you come to the morgue? It'll be easier to show you rather than explain over the phone," Jude said.

Sounded hopeful. They certainly needed a break. "See you in ten," Rachel said.

"Fancy a trip to the morgue? Jude's found something," Rachel said to Jonny.

"Elwyn's been on, he wants more info on Rita Pearce and her husband. He's asking about hospital records, injuries she's sustained, that kind of thing," Jonny replied.

Rachel frowned. She had noticed the bruise. "Okay. If you find anything important, text me. Meanwhile, get photos of her and her family on the board."

Rachel grabbed her things and left the office. Kenton was in the corridor eyeing up the noticeboard. What was he looking for?

"You'll have seen the vacancy for the senior crime officers based in Stockport?" he asked.

"Yes, but why would they be of interest to me?"

"Stockport is closer to your home. It'd be more convenient for you, that's all." He smiled.

Did he want rid of her? The expression on his face gave nothing away, but Rachel felt uncomfortable. "I'm fine where I am, thanks. And if I do decide to move, I'll make the decision without your help." Maybe that was a bit curt, but Rachel found it hard to read this man.

"Ooh, touchy. Get out of the wrong side of the bed?"

Idiot! Who did he think he was? He hadn't been here two minutes and already he was finding her another job. Ignoring him, Rachel walked away, seething. This was only the beginning. Kenton was unlikely to leave things as they were. All his officers at Salford had been hand-picked, they'd joined his team from across the country and had been happy to do so. What mayhem had he planned for her?

* * *

"I hope the way you look is not a reflection of your mood, Rachel," Jude said. "You're obviously troubled. What is it? Do you want to talk about it?"

Rachel inhaled. Jude was more than just a colleague. They'd become close friends over the years. She could trust her. "It's got nothing to do with the case." She paused, and then whispered, "I'm pregnant."

Jude gave her a big smile. "What lovely news! Aren't you pleased?"

"I don't know what I am. I'm confused, torn, unable to decide what I should do about it. And that's all I want to say on the matter."

"That is big news. From the look on your face, I presume it's as much of a surprise to you as it was to me." She put her arm around Rachel. "If you do want to chat, discuss the father, tell me about him, you know where I am."

"Thanks, Jude. Now, let's get on with the job in hand."

Jude led the way into one of the labs. "It'll be tomorrow before I do the full PM, but I've done a preliminary examination and I've found something of interest."

They waited while a technician uncovered the body. "The face is badly decomposed, but he still has hair and most of his teeth. With regard to his ID, you may get a match from dental records. But it was what I found lodged between his back molars that intrigued me." Jude took a kidney dish and showed the contents to Rachel. It contained what looked like fragments of paper. "Odd, don't you think?"

"What is it?" Rachel asked.

"Fragments of bank notes. We've done a little piecing together and there's more than one. It's as if a handful was scrunched up and forced into his mouth."

"Why?"

"That's your province. When you find out, do let me know. It's a first for us." Jude picked up one of the fragments with a pair of tweezers. "This is from a fifty-pound note. We'll run tests on the lot and see if we can decipher any serial numbers. If we do, the bank might be able to help."

Rachel shook her head. "It's a weird one, alright, however the notes got there."

"Jason is doing a fingertip search of that small cellar and the tunnel entrance. I have examined what's left of our victim's legs and I'm fairly certain that he was shot — both knees, I'm afraid. Jason is looking for the bullets.

"You're looking for a nasty bugger, Rachel. I sincerely hope you find him. We've cleaned up the leather jacket too. The letters on the back definitely spell 'Gav.' Short for Gavin?"

There was no one with that name on the list of tenants. "That's something we can use. Thanks, Jude. Oh, and about the other thing. I have told you and Elwyn and that's it. I haven't figured out what to do about it yet, so, well, I'm in denial, I suppose."

"It's a huge decision and not an easy one, but would you consider a termination?"

In the wee small hours of the night, of course she had, but she'd think about that some other time. Rachel didn't want to consider the consequences of the choice. A baby would be inconvenient, it'd put paid to any career move she might have planned, but was that a good enough reason to get rid of it?

"I haven't thought about it, Jude. But I'm going to have to soon. If I do have a termination, no one need ever know. But if I have the baby, then I'll have to tell the father, my girls, and sort my job out. It's too much right now. I'll decide after we've wrapped this case up."

CHAPTER THIRTEEN

By the time Rachel had finished with Jude, it was late, time to call it a day. She rang the station and spoke to Elwyn. "The leather jacket — the name on the back is definitely 'Gav.' In the morning, get Amy to look at the previous tenants, find as many of them as she can and see if they ever employed a Gav or Gavin. There's more, but I'll fill you in tomorrow. I'm beat and need to get home."

"We saw Rita Pearce on the same road as Siddall's bungalow — bit of a coincidence, that. She said she didn't know Andy Siddall — that's who we'd been to see — but she has to be lying. That got me thinking. It could be that the pair are more than just friends. Whatever she said, they have to know each other from the Andy's Auto days. It's one explanation for the bruise on her cheek — a jealous husband."

"All very interesting but it doesn't help the case," Elwyn said.

"It might if the dead man knew and had threatened the pair in some way. Siddall has suffered a serious hand wound in the past and can't use it. I'm wondering if Ray Pearce did that."

Rachel couldn't think about it now. She was done in and needed to rest. Elwyn's speculations were just spinning around in her head. "We'll discuss what it might mean tomorrow."

Rachel left the car park and headed for the A6 — busy at this time of the day. Working in central Manchester had its advantages but it was quite a distance from her home and involved travelling she could do without. Perhaps Kenton had a point. Problem was, Rachel enjoyed working with her team and would be loath to leave them.

An hour later, Rachel pulled into the lane where she lived. It quiet, remote, the semi-detached cottages and a farmhouse were the only properties at this end, and the only one with its lights blazing was hers.

Alan was out in his drive sweeping up leaves. He waved. "I've sold it!" he shouted. "The 'For Sale' sign didn't even go up. One day on the agent's books and it was gone. Apparently the buyer is more than keen, jumped in straight away."

"Well done. Do you have a name for my new neighbour?"

"Not yet, but he's paying cash and isn't bothered about a survey, which is great news given the state of the roof."

"Lucky you. Get your asking price?"

"Yes, so we've put a deposit down on the one in Bollington. Even if my eager buyer pulls out, we can afford it between us. Don't want to miss it, you see. We'll move into Belinda's farm while we wait for our new one."

"Me and the girls will miss you," Rachel said. "It's a big change for all of us."

"I'll be close enough. You need me, just ring."

Rachel knew Alan meant what he said. He'd never faltered in taking responsibility for the girls. She knew how devastated he'd be if it came out that Mia was Jed's and not his. But how long could it remain a secret?

Rachel went indoors. Megan was at the kitchen table working on some university stuff and she could hear Mia on her phone upstairs. There was food cooking — Alan had made pizzas. Problem was, Rachel was off her food and the thought of cheese made her heave.

"Sophie's asked me if I want to share her flat in town," Megan announced. "I haven't said anything to Dad. I thought I'd run it past you first."

Rachel was doubtful. She knew her daughter and her faults. Megan was untidy, forgetful and unused to fending for herself. "Are you sure you'd cope? She lives in a student house. There'd be no food on the table when you got home, no cleaning done, unless you do it, of course. Not to mention all the washing you generate. It doesn't get done by magic, you know."

"Yeah, stop stressing. I'd be fine, don't go on, Mum. Sophie's a good friend and we'd share the chores. What's not to like?"

"Sharing a bathroom, having to shop and cook, not to mention the expense . . . Do I have to say more?" Rachel smiled.

"I've got two years to go at uni. I hate having to trudge into Manchester every day. Please say you don't mind, Mum."

Megan was nineteen and she didn't need Rachel's permission. "Perhaps I can come and have a look at the place? It's a big step, branching out on your own."

Megan heard the doubt in her mother's voice. "You were living away from home at my age. How come it was okay for you but it's not for me?"

Rachel couldn't win this argument. Megan was right. She'd loved her parents but the minute she was able to leave home and go to university, that's what she'd done. Then she'd met Jed McAteer and had never returned. At first, four of them had shared a flat. They'd been good days, carefree and packed with parties. Rachel could well imagine what Megan would get up to.

But Rachel didn't want to think too deeply about all that. In the end, Megan would probably get her own way. Rachel didn't have the energy to fight it. She was tired and all she wanted to do was get to bed. She needed all the rest she could get. Over the coming days, the case would take all her energy and some.

CHAPTER FOURTEEN

Thursday

Amy had looked at the information Mathew Shawcross had given them on the mill tenants and updated it with any changes of address and what they were up to these days.

"As you will see, ma'am, all are working except Andy Siddall. Siddall is registered as disabled due to his hand injury. He was a one-man business but for a while he did employ a man called Gavin Wellburn. We know that from the PAYE records he filed."

Was that the Gav who'd owned the jacket? Scanning the incident board, she could see that Elwyn had already noted that Siddall had said he didn't recognise the name. Rachel wondered why he didn't mention that he'd employed a Gavin. "Do we know what Wellburn did after the job with Siddall finished?"

"No, ma'am. Try as I might, I can't find a single trace of Gavin Wellburn since that time," Amy said. "But I did find his wife. I spoke to her on the phone and asked if we could speak to him. She told me he was missing, but she's not reported it to us and was cagey about why she hadn't."

"That isn't good enough. We'll speak to her again. He was her husband — she must know what happened, why he took off like that. Given his name and that jacket, he could well be our victim. Let's hope his wife decides to be more helpful when two coppers turn up on her doorstep." She turned to Jonny. "Ask around and find out what you can about the drug dealing that's allegedly going on at the mill. See if you can determine how long it's been a problem. The victim could have fallen foul of those involved. Try to get the name of the main man." She turned back to Amy. "Jude is examining the remnants of some banknotes found in the victim's mouth. If she comes up with any serial numbers, get on to the bank."

Rachel made some notes on the board about the latest findings. "Keep me informed about anything you get. Okay, Elwyn, I'll get my jacket, then we'll go."

On the way down the stairs, Elwyn said, "Given what Amy has discovered, it's highly likely that it is Wellburn in the mill, so why didn't his wife report him missing?"

"Knows he's dead, or believes he's still alive somewhere? Doesn't care? Who knows? But one way or another, we want the truth. Time is running out on this, Elwyn. Kenton, remember?"

"She lives in Clayton, not far. I'll drive. You look knackered already," Elwyn said.

"I'm permanently knackered these days. But I do have a lot to think about. Alan's sold the house — cash buyer, looking for a quick sale. If all goes well and there are no legal hiccups, I'll have a new neighbour before long. Hope they're easy-going. They'll need to be, living next door to us lot."

"He's lucky. The market's quiet at the moment. Tell me about the banknotes in the poor victim's mouth."

"They were only fragments, but Jude might get something. She reckons a bunch of them were scrunched up and shoved in." Rachel went quiet for a moment. "What does that say to you, Elwyn?"

"Not sure. An argument among thieves perhaps? One of the gang trying to make off with more than his share?"

"That's what I thought. I've also been wondering if it could have something to do with the drug-dealing we've heard about."

"Let's see what Mrs Wellburn has to say. Our first task is to identify the victim."

* * *

The Wellburns lived in a backstreet of terraced houses in Clayton. Elwyn pulled up outside. "You up for this? You look a bit grey."

"Let's just get on with it," Rachel said wearily. "I might look like crap, but I feel okay."

"That's not what I said. I'm concerned, that's all, Rachel. Anything happens to you or the infant, and your secret's out."

"I am looking after myself, eating regularly and all that. Stop being such an old woman and let's get this done."

Hazel Wellburn answered the door and eyed her visitors with suspicion. "I had a call earlier. You're here about our Gav? What d'you want him for?"

"Is he here?" asked Elwyn

"No, like I told the other one, he's missing. What's he done to bring you lot to my door?"

"Can we come in, Mrs Wellburn?"

She looked warily up and down the street. "No, you can stop out there. It doesn't do to have coppers in the house round here."

"When did you last see Gavin?" Rachel asked her.

"Okay, what's the use, I'm sick of covering his back. Not recently. He's working in Blackpool, so it's been a while. He can't just get time off."

She was being evasive, and Rachel was becoming annoyed. "When exactly, Mrs Wellburn? Last week? Last month? Have you spoken to him on the phone, perhaps?"

"Look, what's all this about? Why don't you lot leave Gav alone? You must have more important stuff to deal with."

Rachel showed the woman the image of the leather jacket on her phone. "Do you recognise this, Mrs Wellburn?"

She nodded. "Course I do, it's Gav's jacket. He had it made by that bloke that worked with leather, he had a unit in a mill in Ancoats."

"Shawcross Mill," Elwyn said.

"Gav used to be a mechanic. He did a couple of private jobs for the leather man, and in return he made him that. Personally, I'd have preferred the money. Bloody jackets don't pay the lecky bill."

"Did Gavin work at the mill?" Rachel asked.

"For a while, at Andy's Autos, but they fell out. Don't know what about, so don't ask."

Elwyn made a note. They now had another link between 'Gav' and the mill. "What did he do after he left the mill?"

"He got a job with a betting shop in Salford."

"But now he's working away?" Elwyn asked.

She shrugged. "His choice."

"We've found a body, Mrs Wellburn," Rachel told her. "In Shawcross Mill. This jacket was with it."

The woman fell silent. After a while, she said, "You think Gav is dead? He can't be."

"We don't know. It would help if you could recall when you last spoke to him."

She looked at Rachel and shook her head. "Truth is, we've split. A divorce costs money we don't have. It's better for us both this way. The job in Blackpool came up and Gav jumped at it. He saw it as a chance to get away for a bit, give us both a chance to think about things."

"When was this?" asked Elwyn.

"Not sure."

"Think, Mrs Wellburn. This is important."

"About three years ago."

Rachel found it incredible that this woman had watched her husband walk away and not tried to make contact. "And you haven't heard from him since?"

"I've had a couple of postcards. He said he's doing well."

Postcards? That didn't sound right. Why not just text or phone? "Do you still have them?"

"No, I binned them. One came about a year after he left and another a few months later." She looked from one detective to the other. "Gav left me. He was probably shacked up with another woman when he sent them — guilty conscience."

Ignoring this, Rachel asked, "How old was Gavin when he left you?"

"Thirty-four."

"Do you have a photo of him we could take?"

She went inside and came back carrying a photo frame. "Me and him at a wedding a few weeks before he did one."

Gavin Wellburn had been tall and well built, with blonde hair. "Do you recall the date you saw Gavin for the last time?" Rachel asked.

"No. I got back from work three years ago and he'd packed his stuff and left. He rang me that night, said he wasn't coming back and that he'd be in touch when he got settled."

"And you accepted that?" Rachel asked.

"We were finished. Why wouldn't I?"

"Did Gav know anyone else at the mill?" Elwyn asked.

"He drank with the mechanic, Andy. They were big mates until they fell out. You should ask him when he last heard from Gav."

CHAPTER FIFTEEN

Rachel looked at the photo. "This might help, I suppose. Who knows?"

"Jude's good but the remains are virtually a skeleton," Elwyn reminded her. "They bear no resemblance to the bloke in that photo."

"We need another word with Andy Siddall. Ring the station, Elwyn, and have him brought in."

They drove back in silence. Rachel was trying to work out what might have happened. The mill had been a busy place, people from those units no doubt went to the Spinners Arms across the road. They would all have known each other. Siddall hadn't admitted to knowing Wellburn. Why was that? He must have drunk in the Spinners Arms with the others. And what about Rita Pearce? "While uniform find Siddall, we'll go and speak to Rita again. Siddall knew Gavin Wellburn — I'd like to know what he and Rita discussed that time she reckoned she didn't visit him."

"She maintained she didn't know Siddall lived there and was visiting a friend. Proving otherwise could be tricky. Let's see what Siddall tells us first."

Elwyn was right. Go charging in and Rita Pearce would clam up. Rachel had seen the woman, she was afraid of something, or someone, and whatever it was meant she didn't want to speak to the police. But it was niggling at her.

At least it looked like they now had a name for their victim.

* * *

Rachel was at her desk checking her inbox when Jonny came in.

"An informant of mine has given me some useful info, ma'am. He maintains that the dealer at the mill is a bloke called Billy Sherwin," Jonny said.

"Is he on the system?" Rachel asked.

Jonny shook his head.

"No record, then. See what else you can discover. And keep me posted."

"Siddall is in interview room two," Elwyn said as Jonny left. "He doesn't look happy."

Rachel got to her feet. "Let's see what he has to say for himself. Jonny's got a lead on a possible dealer. Does the name Billy Sherwin mean anything to you?"

Elwyn shrugged. "No, but all that means is if he is dealing, he's been clever enough to keep his nose clean."

"Difficult if the operation is as big as Healey suggested. We should speak to him too — see how he reacts to the name. If we keep the pressure on, he might talk to us."

"You think the victim fell foul of the dealing operation?" he asked.

"At the moment it's all we've got, Elwyn."

CHAPTER SIXTEEN

The moment they entered the room, an irritable-sounding Siddall began. "You're wasting your time and mine. I've already told you everything I know."

"Not quite," Rachel said. "Tell us about your relationship with Rita Pearce."

"Nothing to tell."

"I don't believe that, Andy. We spoke to the pair of you separately yesterday and it can't have taken you long to swap notes. Rita visited you. What did she want?"

His face reddened and he glared at Rachel angrily. "Leave Rita alone. She's done nothing wrong. She's confused and worried about what's happened, that's all."

"At the first sign of the police, she runs to you. Why is that? Are you two close?"

"I know Rita, course I do," he said. "Most of us from the units used to drink in the Spinners Arms a lot. Rita is a laugh — we all like her. You've been there, you'll have met her husband. The man's a bully, he makes her life a misery and that little witch of a daughter doesn't help. Rita doesn't do as she's told, and she gets a beating. Have you seen her face recently? I've tried to help her in the past, but in truth I only made things worse, so I backed off. That's why we keep our friendship a secret. If Ray finds out you're interested in Rita, he'll kill her."

Without comment, Rachel put the photo of Gavin Wellburn on the table. "What happened to him? His wife told us one version earlier today. What's yours?"

Siddall picked it up and smiled. "You know the truth, then? Okay, I admit I employed Gav briefly, but it didn't work out. This was taken about four years ago. You can see the mill in the background. Is it Gav you've found? Poor sod."

"We're still not sure," said Rachel. "Now you admit that you did know Wellburn, but when we first spoke you said you didn't. Why lie to us, Andy?"

"Because the body you found might not be Gav, you could still be wrong, and I don't want to say anything that'll stop you finding out the truth."

"Rubbish! What are you afraid of?"

"Nothing. If I could tell you anything helpful, I would."

"Suppose for a moment we go with the body being Gavin Wellburn. Do you know why anyone would want to murder him?" Rachel stared at him.

"No, he was a good bloke."

"Do you know of anything about Gavin that would help us to identify him? I'm talking broken bones, dentistry, anything."

Siddall stared at her blankly and then it clicked. "He's too far gone to recognise, isn't he? All you've got is a load of bones and that bloody jacket."

"What d'you mean, *bloody jacket*?" Elwyn asked.

"Never had the thing off his back. We were all in town one night and got into a bit of bother drinking, and then we got into a fight. A bloke ended up in hospital and that's how he fingered us — described Gav's jacket. You lot picked him up on CCTV and brought us all in."

"So you have a record," Rachel said.

"No, the bloke was okay, a few bruises, nothing serious. He dropped the charges."

"You were lucky," said Elwyn. "Who exactly was involved in this altercation?"

"Can't rightly remember . . . me, Gav and Ray Pearce, yeah, that's right."

Elwyn wrote the names down and put a question mark beside them. "Back to DI King's question, is there anything you can think of that will help us confirm it's Gavin?"

"I don't think he ever broke anything, but he was very particular about his teeth. One of the bottom ones at the front got cracked in a rugby match. Gav was aiming for the touchline and went crashing into one of the goalposts, right mess his mouth was."

He had Rachel's full attention. "What did he do about it?"

"Got it fixed. It cost a packet, I know that much. But you'd never know, it looked so real. He had a false one matched to the others then screwed and cemented in. I know he never said anything much to his missus, didn't want her know how much it cost."

"Thanks, Andy, that might be helpful. I'll check it out." Rachel got up to leave. "You can go for now but stay local, we'll be wanting to talk to you again."

Despite what he'd told them, Rachel was sure Siddall was still holding something back. Out in the corridor, she rang Jude on her mobile. "Gavin Wellburn had a false bottom tooth. It appears he wasn't happy with an ordinary false one and had a permanent one fixed."

"I haven't done the X-rays yet, but I'll get on with them at once. If they confirm what you say, I'll ring you. I plan to do the PM this afternoon, if you want to come?"

"Okay, me and Elwyn will see you later." Rachel was beginning to feel better. This could be progress, and they certainly needed it.

Back in the incident room, she looked at the names Siddall, Pearce and Wellburn on the board. Apart from Shawcross Mill, what else linked them? Every instinct told her there was something, but what?

"Ma'am," Jonny said. "Billy Sherwin appears to be on his uppers. I can only find one bank account and that's in the red. He doesn't own any property or a car."

"I hope you got a warrant before you accessed that account. We don't want any comebacks. Amy, anything on those bank notes yet?"

"Forensics only came up with partial serial numbers so the bank says it could take a while."

That was one part of the puzzle Rachel couldn't figure. Why stuff money into a man's mouth before you kill him — and fifties at that? She went to her office to think, but all she could come up with was the falling-out among thieves that they'd spoken about before. But if that was the case, what had been stolen?

Her office phone rang. It was Jason Fox, Jude's colleague.

"We've got the all-clear to examine the tunnel where the body was found. It's quite safe, probably been there for centuries according to the council. Part of an early Victorian sewer, they reckon, extended when the mill was first built."

That was excellent news. There could be evidence down there and if there was, Jason would find it.

CHAPTER SEVENTEEN

"We've cleaned him up," Jude said. "He had blonde hair, if that helps."

"It checks with the description we have of Gavin Wellburn but we need more than that."

Jude nodded. "The X-rays are ready. I'm having them sent down." She joined the pathologist Colin Butterfield at the table.

"The leg bones are broken, and the knee joints shattered by gunshot. It's impossible to determine how the other breaks happened, but they could have been done deliberately or perhaps as a result of being thrown into that space," Butterfield said. "It would help to know where he was shot. That could help determine if he was dead or alive when they bricked him up."

Rachel shivered. Either option was horrific. "How would it help?"

"If the bullets are found where he was, then that's where he was shot. That sort of wound isn't usually intended to kill, but to maim. Therefore, it was the killer's intention that the man suffer. Perhaps until the moment he finally died."

"We'll see what forensics find, but we might never know," Jude pointed out. "His teeth are in good condition.

Taking that and the good state of the joints that are intact, I would put his age at thirty-five to forty."

"I concur," said Butterfield.

"Do you know what killed him?" asked Elwyn.

"There is an indentation on his skull, on the right temple, but the skull itself isn't fractured so I doubt it killed him. Knocked him unconscious, possibly caused an internal bleed, but decomposition makes it impossible to determine. He was shot in both knees and could no longer stand or help himself. He would have bled profusely and, given the head wound, lain unconscious for a while. It's not a nice thought, Rachel, but he could have bled to death, died of hypothermia or even starvation. He was bricked up, remember. The position of that tunnel is such that he could have screamed for days and no one would have heard him."

"You're saying that he could have been alive and just left like that?"

"Yes, Rachel, that's a real possibility," Butterfield said. "Which suggests that whoever did it wanted him to suffer and made certain he couldn't escape."

"Well, they certainly did that," Elwyn said. "The space he was found in was dark and cramped. I find it surprising that anyone even knew it was there."

Elwyn had a point. Rachel could have kicked herself for not thinking of it herself. Whoever did it would have needed a pretty good knowledge of how that mill was built. And that led them straight back to the Shawcross family.

"Do we have any further information about that tunnel?" she asked Jude.

"Jason is still down there. He hasn't reported back yet."

A technician entered the room and handed Jude a large envelope.

"The X-rays." Jude put them up on the viewer. "There's your answer. See the remnants of metal in the lower jawbone?" She pointed. "Even close up, there's nothing to see from the outside. I'd say he was punched quite heavily about the mouth shortly before death, and that broke his lower jaw causing that piece of metal you see to shift to the odd angle it's at now. The false tooth it was attached to has fallen out. If Jason finds it, he'll bring it in."

Rachel took a look at the body — the blonde hair, the right age and the false tooth, along with the distinctive leather jacket. It was enough. They finally had a firm ID for the victim.

"Thanks, Jude. We'd better tell his wife."

* * *

Outside in the car park, Rachel had to stand a minute and take a few deep breaths. Gavin Wellburn had met a dreadful end. Whoever had done that to him had to be brought to book.

"You can leave this to me if you want to get off," Elwyn said. "I'm not insensitive, I saw you were struggling in there. Jude will finish up and send the report through."

"No, I'll stick with it. We'll tell Mrs Wellburn together, then I'll drop you at the station and go home."

"I won't argue. I know you — that'll only get me an earful. But I'll drive so you can take a breather."

Rachel wasn't about to argue that one. It was rush hour, and the traffic along Ashton New Road would be bumper to bumper.

"Now we have to piece it together, find out why Wellburn was killed. Dealing, d'you think?"

"I'm not sure. But the bank notes in his mouth suggest an argument over money. We'll talk to Healey tomorrow and, if needs be, we bring in Billy Sherwin, see what he has to say."

"D'you reckon Wellburn's wife told us the truth?"

Rachel turned away and stared out of the window at the slow-moving traffic. The next bit was the part of the job she hated the most. "What do we say to her, Elwyn? She's bound to ask how he died. There's no way I can give her any of the details from the PM. They might have split, but he was still her husband."

"We say the body we found is Gavin and leave it at that. If she insists, we can direct her to Jude," Elwyn said.

"That's a cop-out, but I'll go with it for now. No details tonight, agreed? I don't have the stomach for it, Elwyn."

CHAPTER EIGHTEEN

Jonny deliberately hung around so that he was last to leave the incident room. He had a plan. Amy had gone off the minute Elwyn told them DCI King wasn't coming back after the PM. He told Jonny to do the same, but the young DC made an excuse about needing to check his emails. "Anything comes in, I'll let you know," Jonny promised.

"In that case I'll do one myself," Elwyn said. "Don't hang around too long. Tomorrow is another day."

True, but dodging the workload wasn't the way to rise through the ranks. Extra effort put in now, while he was a lowly detective constable, wouldn't hurt.

Keen to move the case along, Jonny wanted to know more about the drug dealing around the mill. Healey was involved, for sure, but what about the other unnamed man Healey had hinted at? The name Billy Sherwin had come up before and, despite finding nothing on him, Jonny suspected he was worth a closer look. If Jonny could prove Sherwin was involved, he would be questioned, and it might mean being a step closer to finding whoever killed Wellburn.

Jonny was taking a risk. He was aware that he should have told someone what he was up to, but he reckoned he'd be safe enough, given that the mill was being watched around the clock by a couple of uniformed officers. Anything went wrong, all he had to do was shout.

Jonny left the station and drove to Shawcross Street, parked up in the shadows and waited. There was no one about. The Spinners Arms was lit up, but the windows were small and grimy so there was no chance of seeing who was inside.

He waited almost an hour before a couple of lads approached the mill gates. They saw the two uniforms on duty, spent the next few minutes screaming obscenities at them, then moved on, laughing. Jonny watched them walk to the end of the street and disappear into a ginnel that led to the rear of the mill.

Jonny hopped out of his car and keeping to the shadows, followed the lads at a distance. They had dodged through a hole in the fence and were standing in the mill yard at the back of the building, well out of sight of the uniforms, and given the size of the building, unlikely to be heard either. They were soon joined by a third lad who opened the back gates. The uniforms at the front entrance hadn't got a clue.

Jonny crouched low against the tall, dark walls. Within minutes, the lad at the gate was surrounded by at least a dozen others, all on push bikes. He was handing over small packets from a plastic shopping bag and collecting what Jonny presumed to be cash. Suddenly the entire scene was illuminated by the headlights of a car that had just driven through the opened back gates.

The driver got out. He was a huge brute of a bloke, who towered above the kids. Jonny heard him shouting.

"Stupid idiots, haven't you seen the coppers round the front?" He made for the lad who'd been doling out the packets, picked him up and sent him spinning to the ground, where he landed on his backside.

"Beef! Get off me!" the lad screamed.

Jonny hadn't heard the nickname 'Beef' before, but given the size of the man, he could see why he'd earned it. As Jonny strained his eyes to see what was going on, he suddenly heard a young woman shout into the darkness.

"Leave him, Billy! We need to go."

Billy! So Jonny had been right in his suspicions, Billy Sherwin *was* the top man round here. Jonny watched the girl get out of the car and try to help the lad up off the ground.

"He's banged his head," she shouted. "You hit him too hard!"

"Leave the little bastard alone. He'll be fine. Get back in the car."

"But he's not right," she said. "He can barely stand!"

Sherwin took hold of the girl's arm and dragged her off. "Get in. We've got stuff to do. And you lot, leave this until the police clear off. I swear you haven't a brain cell between you." He cuffed one of the lads on the ear. Jonny could hear the blow. "Get caught and you're on your own. You'll get no help from me."

Jonny stared at the girl, caught in the car headlights. He'd seen her before somewhere. Of course — her photo was up on the incident board. Jasmine Pearce, Rita's daughter.

* * *

Within ten minutes the lot of them had cleared off, leaving the mill as quiet as the grave. On his way back to his car, Jonny was stopped by the two uniforms, who had completely missed the fracas round the back.

Jonny showed them his badge. "DC Farrell from East Manchester CID," he said. "We're investigating the murder."

"We heard a noise," one of the PCs said.

"Just kids. They've gone now." Jonny decided to keep what had just gone on to himself. That was for the team to deal with in the morning. He made for the Spinners Arms. If she was in the right mood, Rita Pearce might just talk to him. On his way across the road, he debated whether to tell her about Jasmine.

Rita was behind the bar, drying glasses. She recognised him the minute he walked through the door. "You work with that detective," she said. "Look, I'm tired of all this. What do you want now?"

"A coke." Smiling, Jonny looked around. There were only four people in the pub and one of them was Dylan Healey. He was seated on his own by the window.

"I got bail, copper," he shouted across. "I've also got a good lawyer, so you'll be lucky to pin this one on me."

"We don't pin things on anybody, Dylan," Jonny said. "We gather evidence and go from there. And given the evidence we're gathering on you, you'll need the best when you go in front of a judge."

Healey scowled and took a swig of his lager.

"Has Beef been in tonight? I saw the car across the road," Jonny said.

Healey looked surprised. "You know Beef, then?"

"Yeah, we do a little business now and again," Jonny lied. You never knew, Healey might let something slip if his guard was down.

But Rita interrupted the conversation. "You've said enough. At this rate I'll get a brick through the window. Get out, Dylan, and stay out until you're sorted." She turned to Jonny. "You don't fool me. I doubt you've ever spoken to the man. And you're wasting your time anyway. Beef Sherwin doesn't come in here unless he has to."

"Not even to see your daughter?" Jonny asked.

Rita looked horrified. "Shut your mouth. Don't go shouting his name in my pub again. Talk to you lot about that animal and it brings a load of trouble to your door."

She marched across and collected Healey's empty glass. Jonny drained his coke. Rita Pearce wasn't going to talk to him, but at least he knew for sure that Sherwin was involved in the dealing. Is that why Wellburn was killed? Had he double-crossed Sherwin?

CHAPTER NINETEEN

Friday

First thing Friday morning, Dylan Healey was back at the station. Rachel decided she'd interview him with Jonny. The young DC had done his homework on the dealing at the mill and knew the score. Not that she was happy with him going it alone.

"I thought we'd had this conversation before," she said. "You do recall the Danulescu debacle?" She was referring to Jonny's solo performance in an earlier case. "You went off alone then, too, and nearly got yourself killed."

"With respect, last night was a risk worth taking, ma'am. There were a couple of uniformed officers at the front, so all I had to do was shout."

"But they were oblivious to what was going on at the back of the mill?"

"Yes, but it is a big building and those kids weren't daft, they kept relatively quiet."

"You saw Sherwin?"

"I saw a bloke drive up in a fancy car. I took the registration number and checked it out this morning. It does belong to Billy Sherwin as I suspected, but what surprised me was seeing Jasmine Pearce with him."

Rachel inhaled. She didn't fancy telling Rita Pearce that her daughter was running drugs. She'd been reasonably helpful so far, but this was something else.

"I reckon if we present Healey with the facts, he'll crack. He'll be too scared that Sherwin will think he grassed," Jonny said.

"But he wasn't involved in whatever was going down at the mill last night. He was in the pub, drinking, you said. It would have made more sense if he'd met Sherwin or been the one organising those kids. And you were on your own, remember. It's your word against Sherwin's that he was even there at all. Healey is treated with kid gloves until we get some positive answers," she said firmly. "Have you got that, Jonny? We don't upset him. If we want Sherwin, then Healey must tell us about him."

"When Healey spoke to us before, the drug boss he was referring to was Sherwin. Has to be. One of his gang or not, he knows a lot more than he's told us."

Jonny might be right. Rachel hated interviewing suspects under these conditions. They were forced to rely on Healey telling them the truth, and he had a lot to lose if he did.

* * *

Dylan Healey was sitting next to the duty solicitor, sipping water, when they went in. He smiled at the two detectives as if they were old friends.

"Could do with sprucing up a bit, this place. I'm not too fond of the insipid green paint. It's peeling off the walls over there."

Ignoring this remark, Rachel smiled benignly. "Morning, Dylan. We appreciate you coming in. Hope we're not keeping you from anything important."

"I had a skinful last night. You're lucky I'm out of my pit."

"In that case, we'll try to wrap this up quickly. Tell us about Billy Sherwin," she said.

"Or perhaps you know him better as Beef." Jonny, too, was smiling. "I can see why you'd be scared of him, a man that size."

This made Healey defensive. "I hardly know the bloke. See him about sometimes. I think he's going out with some bird who lives in a flat near me."

"I think you know very well who Sherwin is, and how he makes his money. He's the supplier, the main man selling drugs from the mill. Does he supply you, Dylan?"

Healey stared at Rachel. "No. What makes you think Sherwin's got owt to do with drugs anyway?"

"I've had a tip-off," she said, which wasn't a lie. Still, Healey didn't have to know it was Jonny who'd told her. "What's the set-up? Billy Sherwin sources the drugs that get handed out to the lads who distribute for him — including you, I imagine. He must be raking in a fortune."

That made him agitated. "You can't go spreading that around, I won't make it to the end of the day. Who told you anyway? You can't go saying it was me. Word gets around and I'll end up with a bullet in my head."

"Nasty," Rachel said. "You should choose your friends with more care."

"I don't know anything, copper. Can't help you."

He definitely looked frightened. Billy Sherwin's name certainly carried some clout. "If you speak to us, Dylan, we can help you. We'll find you a safe place to stay until this is all over. We'll protect you."

Healey went silent. Was he considering the offer?

"You live alone, you don't have a family to support. The CPS would look at the current charge of assault more favourably if we told them you were helping us."

His head shot up. "You mean I wouldn't go to prison?"

"I can't promise, you understand, but it can only help your case."

Healey looked at his brief. "What d'you think?"

Until this moment, the solicitor had said nothing, simply sat and taken notes. Now he whispered into Healey's ear.

"He says I should take up the offer. But I'm not sure. You don't know these people like I do."

The solicitor shook his head.

"It's alright for you lot, but my life's round here. What am I supposed to do when you move me?" Healey asked.

"It doesn't have to be for good, just until we've arrested and charged Sherwin. No one will find you. Tell us what we need to know, and we'll do the rest," Rachel said.

"You're sure? Billy Sherwin won't find out?"

"Not unless you tell him," Jonny said.

"Can I think about it? Dobbing someone in is a big deal for me. Sherwin's clever and he's tough. He has people everywhere. Cross him and you're dead."

"Has that ever happened before?" Rachel asked. "Has anyone ever been brave enough to take him on?"

"Some men did a while ago. Didn't get them anywhere though. Beef hurt one of 'em real bad. I haven't seen any of them since."

"Who were these men?"

"Don't know their names, just some blokes who tried to stop him."

Rachel looked at Jonny. This could be the answer. Some of the men working in the units had got in the way of Sherwin's business and Wellburn had paid the price.

"Tell me about his girlfriend," Rachel said.

"What girlfriend?"

"Jaz, that girl from the pub. She helps him," Jonny said.

"She's not his girlfriend. Beef goes about with some posh bird."

"And Jasmine?" Rachel asked.

"I've no idea. Perhaps Beef has a hold over her, perhaps she's a junkie. There are others who I don't know. He's one clever operator, is Sherwin. He runs a chain of people, but no one 'cept him knows who they all are."

"A few names, and dates. That's all we're asking for, Dylan. No one will know we got them from you," Rachel said.

"Give us some paper and a pen."

Jonny passed them over and Healey began to write.

He sat back. "That's all you're getting. Can I go now?"

CHAPTER TWENTY

Back in the incident room, Rachel gathered the team together. "The man we want is one Billy Sherwin, nickname, Beef. Find him and bring him in."

"What about his girlfriend, Jasmine Pearce?" Elwyn asked.

Jonny piped up. "It's a weird one, that. I wonder how much her mother knows."

Just then, Amy interrupted them. "Ma'am, Dr Fox has been on. He's found something interesting at the mill."

"Jonny, get an address for Sherwin and organise bringing him in. Amy, get some background on him. We've looked at his bank records and found nothing. Get a warrant and we'll take a look at what Jasmine Pearce has stashed away."

Rachel turned to Elwyn, who was already logging out of his computer. "You and me will go and see what Jason's found. With luck, it'll be something useful."

Kenton called to her from the doorway. "Rachel, a word."

What now? They were going as fast as they could. "We're about to leave — important find down at the mill," she said.

"Still chasing shadows, I see. Isn't it about time you handed the lot over to the cold case team?"

"No, because the murder relates to a current case, one of drug dealing. We think the victim fell foul of the main man and was killed."

"You mean this dealing has been going on for the last three years?" he asked.

"Possibly. He's hardly going to tell us."

"And this station knew nothing about it, even though it's on your patch?"

"The man running things is clever and vicious. No one will speak out against him. However, we've arrested someone who is prepared to give us the whole story — names, suppliers, everything. As part of this investigation, we will find out what happened to our victim, Gavin Wellburn."

Kenton mulled this over. "Forensics costs are through the roof," he said finally. "You've currently got Dr Fox working full time for this department."

"I'm sorry, Mark, but we're gathering evidence. What Jason is doing will prove vital in getting the case past the CPS."

"This time next week and no later. Got that?"

Without replying, Rachel stalked off down the corridor.

In the car park, Rachel climbed in beside Elwyn and slammed the car door. Her face was red, her hands shaking. "Kenton's at it again, going on about the budget. Wants this one wrapping up quick, forensics costs are killing him. How are we supposed to do the damn job?"

"You need to calm down, for starters. Ignore the man. He'll see sense when we get results. He's new on the job. No doubt he's got to impress those higher up the ladder."

"Well he doesn't impress me, that's for sure."

* * *

Because of what had happened the previous night, there was an increased police presence at the mill. There'd be no more dealing here for the foreseeable. Jason Fox greeted her at the entrance, coughing and dusting down his blue forensics suit.

"God, it's foul down there, and the air is still dusty," Jason said.

"I'm not surprised, given the length of time the body was lying there," Elwyn said.

"Which bit are you working on?" Rachel asked.

"The tunnel, and it's interesting. At first, we thought it was built as an overflow for the canal or part of the sewage system for the mill, but we were wrong, it's neither," Jason said.

Rachel couldn't think of anything else it could be. "You're sure? You've checked the old maps?"

"Of course, but they weren't much help, to be honest. Then I got hold of an even older map from the local history section at the library. That's when I spotted it. Come inside and I'll show you."

Pinned to the wall of the huge weaving shed was a copy of an old map, on which Jason had highlighted a route out of the mill and into the streets of Ancoats.

"This is the space where Wellburn was found, and here's the tunnel entrance," Jason said. "The tunnel has been in existence since the mill was built. It's narrow but tall enough to walk down — just. That's what made me think that it wasn't a Victorian sewer."

"So, what is it?" asked Elwyn.

"A shortcut." Smiling, Jason pointed to a spot on the map. "Jeffries Brickyard was over there, way back in the early eighteen hundreds — they made all the bricks that built the mill. It took a hell of a lot, you just need to look at the place to see that. The mill is here." He jabbed a finger at the map. "Without the tunnel, the bricks would have had to be carted by road all the way round. Use the tunnel and the journey was much shorter and more direct."

That made sense. "Who would know it was here?" Rachel asked.

"Without doing the research, very few people. Perhaps the Shawcross family, given that it's their mill, but possibly not even them."

Given where Wellburn's body had been found, the killer must have known it was there too. But how?

"The tunnel was bricked up relatively recently, perhaps after Wellburn was killed. It wasn't a good job, either, the cement was mixed wrong, which is why those two kids were able to break through it."

"Do you think the killer used that tunnel for some other reason, and decided it was the perfect place to hide a body?"

"I don't know, but we need to search the whole thing."

"Okay, but I've already got Kenton on my back about expenses."

"I do have some good news." Jason smiled. "I've found the missing tooth."

CHAPTER TWENTY-ONE

Back at the station, Rachel searched the system for Billy Sherwin and found all she needed to know. He had a record going back years, but not a single conviction. Puzzling, considering the man was extremely violent and had no regard for the law. Reading between the lines of the various reports, Rachel realised that he was still free because he employed excellent lawyers, and because he ran his gang with an iron fist. He was never short of gang members who could be persuaded to admit guilt and so allow Sherwin to walk free. Each time he'd been arrested, and evidence produced, a hapless gang member had come forward and put their hand up. Some had got long sentences. Rachel had to presume that was preferable to crossing a vengeful Sherwin.

"Billy Sherwin has been operating around Shawcross Mill for a while. The tenants of those units must have known about the dealing. I suspect Sherwin will have given them a hard time. Some will have bought from him, perhaps owed him money." Rachel looked at Amy. "Organise uniform to have a word with as many of them as you can find — and get statements."

Amy nodded. "I'll start with Siddall."

"Speak to him, by all means, but don't forget the others. Elwyn, get uniform round to Billy Sherwin's place and bring him in. Make sure there's plenty of back-up. Once he's been processed, you and me will interview him."

Rachel's mobile rang. She glanced at the screen and her stomach flipped — it was Jed. She'd have to take this in her office.

* * *

"You've gone quiet again, not a word since Spain," Jed began. "You know that worries me, given the job you do."

His deep voice sent a shiver of pleasure down her spine, as it always had, but she'd been dreading his call. What to tell him? Not the truth about the baby — she wasn't ready for that yet. She had no alternative but to trot out the usual excuse.

"Work is heavy at the moment — you know how it is. We're in the middle of a complex case and working long hours."

"I thought we'd reached a new understanding after Malaga. I thought we'd talk more, share stuff."

Malaga, and the time they'd spent together, something else that gave her the shivers. It had been an idyllic few days and she'd loved being with him. "And we will. Everything's fine, Jed, don't stress."

"Are the girls okay?"

"Yes, they're both fine — driving me crazy as usual." She was still clutching the reports on Sherwin. She needed to read through them thoroughly before the interview. "Look, Jed, it's good to hear from you, but I can't talk right now. We've got a suspect coming in for interview and I've got to prepare."

"Have dinner with me later. As you know, there is something we should discuss."

Rachel felt her pulse race. What did he mean by *as you know*? What had he found out? Surely not about the baby? "Tonight? I . . . I'm not sure. I've not told the girls or made any arrangements with Alan."

"What we have to discuss is important to us both. The girls are old enough to fend for themselves. I'll take you to that place you like on Deansgate, the one with the Art Deco interior."

"Expensive, and unwarranted. I'm perfectly happy with a sandwich across the road."

"Well, I'm not. I'll pick you up outside the station at seven, and no excuses. We need to have a serious talk about the future. I'm not stupid, Rachel, I've known you too long to be fobbed off with tales of how much work you've got to do."

"Ok, see you later." Rachel heaved a long sigh. He must know. Everything he said pointed that way. But that was a ridiculous idea. How could he know? Her pregnancy was a secret. Nonetheless, there was something on his mind that concerned them both, he'd said. And that scared her. What if he asked outright? There was no way she could lie to Jed. He'd dig and dig until he got to the truth anyway. This wasn't how she wanted it to be.

Rachel returned to the main office looking for Elwyn. She needed a sounding board, someone to give her advice. "Fancy a coffee?" she asked him.

"Problem?"

"Sort of." They went downstairs to the canteen. "Jed wants to take me out this evening, he wants to talk. God knows how, but I think he knows about the baby. But I've not seen him since Spain, Elwyn, so what's happened?"

"Kenton, that's what. You said yourself that they'd seen each other recently."

"Kenton doesn't know either. I've said nothing about the baby to anyone other than you and Jude."

"It's not that, then. He must want to see you about something else."

"There is nothing else."

"Tonight, you say. Shame, you'll miss my housewarming."

Rachel felt awful, she'd completely forgotten about it. "Sorry Elwyn, baby brain," she apologised.

CHAPTER TWENTY-TWO

Amy wasn't happy at being given another behind-the-scenes task while Jonny was out there at the sharp end of this case. He was working hard, chasing promotion, which wasn't a bad idea, but if there was promotion going, then she fancied it for herself.

She studied the list of ten tenants. They were all still in the area. It meant tramping around to each one, hoping to catch them in. Amy decided to pass the task to uniform. They were welcome to it. Siddall, on the other hand, was a sure bet. He didn't work and there was every chance he'd be at home. Amy decided to speak to him first and then Rita Pearce. Sherwin was bound to have drunk in the Spinners Arms — after all, Healey did — and the two knew each other.

Amy took a uniformed constable with her, a fresh-faced young man called Jordan Hamilton, who she knew fancied her. It'd be a little light entertainment for the ride round.

"Our Sergeant Pryce is having a housewarming party tonight. Coming?" she asked him.

"Dunno. He issued a blanket invite in the incident room, but I don't know anyone. I've only been in the job two minutes."

Amy laughed. "You should come. I wouldn't worry about not knowing folk, we're a friendly lot. All except stuck-up DCI King, that is. She's particular who she takes under her wing. Currently it's Jonny Farrell who's her favourite."

Hands on the steering wheel, Jordan flushed. Amy realised he didn't know how to reply. Probably afraid to say anything against King. She laughed and punched his arm. "Don't take any notice, I'm only winding you up. King's okay in small doses."

"I'm hoping to make CID myself one day," he said. "I don't want to stand on too many toes. Perhaps I should go tonight, get to know everyone."

"Come along with me, if you want. We can meet up somewhere first and go in together. Give them all something to gossip about."

He glanced at her and flushed again. "You really wouldn't mind? Turning up with me?"

"No, Jordan. Like I said, it'll get the tongues wagging."

"I only live down the road from the station. I could pick you up if you like," he said.

But Amy didn't want that. Better to meet him on neutral ground. "I'll meet you at the pub on the corner of Elwyn's road. Be there at eight," she said firmly.

The crescent where Siddall lived was quiet, with no one about, not even a twitching curtain. When they parked outside, Amy looked at Jordan and shook her head. "Something's not right, can't you feel it? This place is giving me the creeps. I know it doesn't look like anything's going on, but it still feels as if there's eyes watching us from everywhere."

The door to Siddall's place was ajar. Jordan gave it a gentle push and called out, "Mr Siddall? Are you in?" There was no reply.

"Look." Amy pointed to the hall carpet. It was stained with blood. "I don't like this." She tiptoed through the sitting room, taking care to avoid the blood, and into the kitchen. Pans and broken crockery lay strewn all over the place.

"What d'you reckon happened?" Jordan asked.

"I'd say a fight," Amy said. "And someone's been badly injured if the amount of blood is anything to go by."

"What do we do?" Jordan asked.

"I'll have a look round, see if I can find Siddall. Stay here and don't let anyone else enter. Call it in to the incident room."

Amy had a good look in every room but there was no sign of Andy Siddall. While Jordan was busy phoning the station, she went to see the neighbours and ask if they'd heard anything.

Amy knocked on the house next door. No answer. It was the same all along the row. No one wanted to know, no one wanted to get involved.

"Stella is trying the hospitals," Jordan called to her. "Siddall's not here, so hopefully someone got him help — if he's still alive."

"We need forensics here. There's a lot of blood, Jordan. If Siddall ended up in hospital someone must have called for help or taken him there."

"Who, though?"

"He's pretty pally with Rita Pearce, by all accounts. Perhaps we should try her."

Amy's mobile rang. It was Rachel. "We've found him," she said straight away. "He's in intensive care at the Royal Infirmary."

"How did he get there?"

"An anonymous call from a woman. I'm sending Jonny and forensics to his place, they'll take over. When they get there, you come back to the station. When Jonny's done, he'll go and have a word with Rita Pearce, see what she's been up to this afternoon." Rachel ended the call.

"Bloody Jonny again!" Amy growled. "He gets to see this through while I do the background slog! I'm telling you, Jordan, if you do make it to CID, make sure you watch your back."

CHAPTER TWENTY-THREE

Billy Sherwin's bulk filled the doorway of the interview room, making the two PCs escorting him look positively diminutive. Rachel could see why he'd earned the nickname Beef. He was huge, as wide as he was tall. With his shaven hair and the tattoos up his arms and neck, he looked every bit as intimidating as his reputation suggested.

Once he and his solicitor were seated, Rachel began. "Do you know why you're here, Billy?"

Slouched over the table, he shrugged. "No idea, love, but you'd better get on with it. Things to do, you know how it is."

"I have a witness who's told us that you've been using Shawcross Mill as a base for dealing drugs. What d'you have to say about that, Billy?"

"Nonsense!" he said dismissively. "Never been near the place. Who's been spreading this tripe?"

His indignation cut no ice with Rachel. He might not appear concerned about the allegation but with Healey willing to give evidence, she was holding all the cards. "We've got dates, and the names of the kids you use to deliver for you. Proper little empire you've built."

He laughed. "It's a bloody conspiracy, that's what it is. They've got me confused with someone else."

She smiled. "I doubt that, Billy. You're not someone a person forgets."

"Who? Come on, who's told you this fairy tale?"

Rachel watched his eyes narrow as he tried to work out who'd dared to cross him.

Suddenly he bellowed with laughter. "Spider! It's that stupid scrote, isn't it? You should see your faces. Well, he's having you on. You don't actually believe that lying toerag?"

Rachel smiled back. "He tells such a convincing story, what else can we do but take him seriously?"

"Dates, you said. Okay, give you some dates and I'll tell you where I was. Check it all out. You'll see I'm telling the truth."

"Instead of wasting everyone's time, including yours, Billy, why not simply tell us the truth? And while you're at it, tell us who your supplier is. That sort of information can help someone in your predicament."

"Sod off! You'll get nowt off me other than alibis for them dates you spoke of."

"Okay, Billy, if that's how you want to play this. But you should speak to your solicitor and reconsider. Help us and we'll be in a position to help you."

Rachel got up and left. Back in the incident room, she arranged for the information about the dates to be got from Sherwin.

"These are delaying tactics," Elwyn said. "Healey's given us a list of some of Sherwin's dealings and the youngsters he uses. Sherwin gives us his version, and we chase our tails."

"Even so, everything Sherwin tells us will have to be checked out."

"And in the meantime, does he get bail?"

"Certainly not! We apply for an extension if necessary. I want everyone checking his alibis, all weekend if that's what it takes."

* * *

DC Jonny Farrell was waiting in the corridor outside one of the intensive care rooms at the Manchester Royal Infirmary. There was no way he could speak to Andy Siddall — the doctors had put him into an induced coma.

"He's lost a lot of blood," a nurse told him. "And then there was the head injury. A doctor will be along shortly, he'll be able to tell you more."

"The paramedics who brought him in, are they here, by any chance?"

"I shouldn't think so, but I'll ask."

Jonny wanted information about who had found Siddall and rung for help. 'A woman,' was all he knew. What was the betting that woman was Rita Pearce?

Jonny decided he'd hang around, see who, if anyone, visited. "Is it alright if I stay a while?"

"Be our guest." The nurse smiled. "But he won't be waking up anytime soon."

Jonny settled down on a chair in the corridor. Two uniforms were also on duty, watching. Someone had tried to kill Siddall and failed. They had to acknowledge the possibility that they might try again.

A woman's voice broke into his thoughts. "You were asking about the paramedics who brought that bloke in. I'm Sandra Hale. It was me and my partner."

Jonny stood up and showed the paramedic his badge. "Did you see anyone else near his place?" he asked her.

"We know it was a woman who rang it in. She told the operator at control that she'd found him lying on the kitchen floor and that he'd been shot. She didn't hang around, I'm afraid, said the bare minimum. When we arrived at the bungalow, he was on his own. However, the woman had tried to help him. The bullet went in through his side and lodged in his back. He was bleeding profusely. She'd turned him on his other side and put a cushion under the bleed. It helped stem the flow."

"I don't suppose she gave her name?"

"Afraid not."

CHAPTER TWENTY-FOUR

Rachel kept a spare dress and a pair of heels in the cupboard in her office for those occasions when she was going out straight after work. It was nothing special, a fitted number in her favourite shade of green that she'd worn many times before. Well, it'd have to do. There was no way she could go home, change, and be back in time for the meal with Jed.

She dressed in the ladies' toilet, taking a few minutes to weigh up her reflection in the full-length mirror. The dress was a little tight and showed her swelling belly. She'd have to hope that Jed didn't notice and ask any awkward questions. Then again, if she was right and he already knew, what did it matter? The time was fast approaching when she wouldn't be able to hide the pregnancy from anyone. It was a problem she immediately shelved for another time. At least her hair looked good. She pulled it loose from the scraped-back pony-tail and fluffed it around her face. The colour seemed more vibrant than usual and it looked thicker. Pregnancy did have one or two advantages.

Rachel returned to the office in time to catch Elwyn preparing for the off.

"I'm leaving," he said. "Ffion is at mine sorting the food and folk have started arriving already. You know what they're like around here when there's free food and drink on offer. Shame you can't come."

"Depending on how it goes with Jed, I might pop in later."

"Bet you don't. After dinner, Jed will whisk you off to some posh hotel."

Rachel ran a hand over her belly. "No, he bloody well won't! He's done enough as it is!"

"Whatever happens, don't be confrontational. You can do without the aggro. Remember, it's his baby too."

As if she needed reminding. She wished Elwyn luck with the party, pulled her coat over her shoulders and left the office. Out on the main street it was dark, and the roads were busy with traffic. She didn't have long to wait before she heard a car horn blast and Jed pulled up beside her.

As soon as Rachel was in the passenger seat, he leaned across and kissed her cheek. "Hi," he said softly. "I'd almost forgotten what you looked like."

It was meant as a joke, but it annoyed her. Unreasonable, she knew, but she couldn't help it. She loved Jed, but he always somehow managed to wind her up.

"Don't start, Jed. I've been busy. I told you, work stuff."

"In that case it'll do you good to relax a little. I've booked the table, and we'll go from there."

"Don't get your hopes up. After we've eaten, I'll be going straight home," she told him firmly. "I'm working on a heavy case and I need all the rest I can get."

She saw his expression change — he was trying to control his anger. "What's made you so irritable, Rachel? Surely not the prospect of an evening with me? I had hoped that after Spain, we'd got past that."

Now she felt ashamed. She'd been unreasonable, but she couldn't help being off with him. Her feelings for Jed always brought out the worst in her. Why that was, she'd no idea. Perhaps Elwyn was right in saying it was because she was afraid of showing her true feelings and so resorted to picking at him.

They were stuck at traffic lights. Jed was tapping his fingers on the steering wheel, waiting for them to change.

"Sorry. I know I'm a moody cow. It's been a long day, and I shouldn't take it out on you," Rachel said.

"It's more than that, though. You forget how well I know you." He turned and took a long hard look at her. "You do look a bit peaky tonight. Everything okay? You're not sickening for something?"

Rachel could almost feel his eyes boring into her. "Stop staring at me like that. I'm fine."

"Are you sure? I can drive you home if you'd rather."

So, he didn't know about her condition, because if he did, the attitude and the conversation would have been very different. This wasn't going to be the difficult meeting she'd anticipated, but if it wasn't about the baby, why did he want to see her so urgently?

"What's tonight all about, Jed?" she asked.

"Do I need a reason to take you out? You're the woman I love, or have you forgotten that? We've been close in the past and we should be together now. You know that as much as I do. I don't understand why you persist in fighting me all the way."

If Rachel was honest with herself, she didn't understand either. He had a dubious past, she couldn't forget that, but that was behind him now. But let Jed into her life full time and things would change, not necessarily for the better. She might love him, but could she live with him? "You haven't answered the question."

"I'll tell you shortly, when we're sitting down with people around us." He smiled. "Otherwise, you might hit me."

Not having seen him since Spain, Rachel had no idea what had been going on in his life. "That bad?" She grinned. "Want to give me a clue?

"No, you'll have to wait."

* * *

Jonny paced the corridor outside Siddall's room. Given he was in a coma, there was no chance of speaking to him. But there was always the chance that someone would visit — Rita Pearce, if his suspicions were right. Jonny had left word with the ward sister that if anyone asked, she was to direct them to him.

It was late and apart from the regular beep of the machinery keeping Siddall alive, the ward was eerily silent, the lights dim. Jonny had let the uniforms go to the canteen while they could. It would be a long night for them. He checked his phone. Another ten minutes and then he'd call it a night and get round to Elwyn's.

Someone called to him. "Mr Farrell, someone left this for you at the main desk." The nurse gave him an envelope.

"Male or female?"

"A girl, skinny and tall. She asked about Mr Siddall and then handed this in."

Jonny tore the envelope open. The name on the bottom was Rita Pearce. He'd been waiting for something like this. It seemed to confirm there was something going on between the pair of them. Rita would be running the pub and must have asked Jasmine to deliver the note.

Rita wrote that if he wanted to know who had assaulted Andy Siddall, he'd have to meet her at the pub within the hour.

One of the two PCs returned, so Jonny had a quick word and left them to it. This was too good an opportunity to miss. Rita knew more about Gavin Wellburn than she was saying. Her daughter, Jasmine, was friendly with Sherwin and mixed up in the drug dealing. He hoped that after the assault, one or both would speak to him.

On the way to the car park he rang Amy. "You at Elwyn's yet?"

"Just leaving, why?"

"Rita Pearce wants to talk to me. I'm off to the Spinners Arms for a chat."

"You want me to join you?"

"No, get off to Elwyn's. Tell him I'll be late, would you? I just wanted someone to know where I'd gone, that's all."

"You sure? I can ride shotgun, get your back."

"I'll be fine. See you later."

CHAPTER TWENTY-FIVE

"You haven't eaten much, just sat there and picked at the food. Is there a problem?" Jed asked.

"It's fine. I've been snacking all day," Rachel lied, "now I've no appetite." A lame excuse, the food was exquisite, but the fact was, she was off meat. She couldn't tell him the fillet steak he'd ordered for them, rare, and leaking blood on to the serving plate, was turning her stomach. It was her favourite, he knew that, which was why he'd ordered it. Normally she would have wolfed it down, but now all it did was make her feel sick. Rachel had been the same with the other two — off meat for the duration.

"You haven't had any of the wine either. What's wrong?"

She smiled. "I need to keep a clear head. Besides, I have to drive home."

He sighed. This wasn't going well. Rachel knew she shouldn't have agreed to meet him.

"Come on then," she said, "what's your news? Why all the secrecy?"

"It's pretty big and I'm not sure you'll like it, but you need to know."

Rachel was intrigued. "Don't be such a wimp, just tell me."

"I'm moving out of town. I've put my apartment on the market and bought a house in the Cheshire countryside."

Rachel gave a little whistle. "That's a huge change from what you're used to, Jed. There are no clubs or fancy restaurants out in the sticks, you know. Where I live, it's a hike and a half to the nearest pub." He said nothing. "Give me a clue, then. Where exactly are you moving to?"

"You really don't know? I'm surprised no one has told you."

Who'd be in a position to do that? she wondered. Kenton? "You told Mark before me, is that what you're getting at? My, the pair of you are pally."

"No, not Mark," he said. "Someone a lot closer to you."

He was watching her, waiting for the penny to drop. Rachel usually had a sharp mind, but recently it was as if her head was full of cotton wool.

Finally, he said, "I couldn't resist. It's a delightful cottage, smaller than I'd like but if we put our heads together there is plenty of scope to extend."

Rachel shook her head. "Put our heads together? What am I missing?" she asked. "And why are you grinning?"

Jed took hold of her hand. "You really are off your game, Rachel. I've dropped enough clues by now. Can't you guess?"

She looked up from her seemingly bottomless plate of food, caught his eye and suddenly understood.

"You!" she exclaimed. "You are Alan's cash buyer, my new neighbour!"

"Well done, you got there at last."

Alan wouldn't dare do this to her! Would he? Was this his twisted revenge for never properly explaining how Jed fitted into her life?

Rachel knew Alan was aware that there was something between Jed and her, but he'd never had the courage to ask what. In the early days when she and Alan had got together, Jed had been a shadow in her life, and one she refused to acknowledge. And it had worked, up to a point. But the memory of what she had had with Jed persisted, eventually sounding the death knell for her relationship with Alan.

Alan King was not a stupid man. On the rare occasions he'd met Jed, seen him and Rachel together, the spark had been obvious. But with Belinda on his arm, it seemed Alan no longer cared, so long as he got the sale he needed.

This would change everything. "You can't do this! What about the girls?"

"What about them?" Jed said. "Mia is happy about the move. We've already talked it over."

She could barely believe it. They'd discussed this behind her back! "How dare you! You should have told me first, not Mia. She's a child, only fourteen. She doesn't know what's good for her."

"I'm her father, Rachel," he said, "and I want in before she gets much older. You have no right to stand in the way of our relationship."

"I have every right. You don't have a relationship, other than when it suits you," she spat back. "Alan is Mia's father, not you and I don't intend to tell him or her anything different. You need to think again, Jed. The prospect of having you as a neighbour is nothing short of a nightmare!"

Jed would not be reliable like Alan had been. Alan understood her work and her crazy shift patterns and was willing to stand in and take care of the girls at a moment's notice. Granted, Megan was thinking of moving out, but it hadn't happened yet, and even if she did, she'd be back before long. Rachel couldn't imagine Jed throwing together a lasagne or kneading pizza dough, or putting up with Megan's moods, for that matter.

"Sorry, Jed, I need to think. This is too much to take in. We'll speak later in the week."

Rachel got to her feet, grabbed her coat and marched out of the restaurant. Her eyes full of tears, she walked aimlessly down Deansgate. She should call a taxi, return to the station, get her car and go home, but she couldn't face the drive.

"Mrs King? Rachel?" Someone called from ahead.

Rachel looked up to see who'd spoken. It was a young man, mid-twenties, tall with dark hair mostly hidden under a baseball cap. He was wearing jeans, trainers and a zipped hooded jacket. He blocked her path, shuffling from foot to foot, while Rachel tried to get past him.

"Get out of my way," she ordered.

"Hang on. You should listen. You'll find what I've got to say interesting."

She stared at him. His clothing was dark, except for the trainers, which had vivid yellow-and-red stripes down the sides. "Do I know you?"

He shook his head. "No, but I know you. Your parents were Celia and Richard. Do you know what really happened the night they died?"

Of course she did, but who was this young man? Rachel didn't know how to respond. Who the hell was he? Why this about her parents now? She looked closer but still didn't recognise him.

"Who are you?"

"Not important, Rachel. What is important, however, is that you know the truth about what happened that night."

"I know what happened, and I don't need you raking it up. They were both killed in a car crash, a horrendous accident."

He smiled. "You're wrong, Rachel. I think you should know that crash was no accident, it was engineered."

Having said his piece, he was gone, running like the wind down Deansgate. Rachel could only stare after him as he turned into a passageway and disappeared.

CHAPTER TWENTY-SIX

Shawcross Street was quiet, the mill a black hulk in the darkness. There were no kids to be seen. The police presence, plus Sherwin being in custody, was working. A chat with Rita Pearce was long overdue, in Jonny's opinion. She'd attended A & E five times in the past two years with various injuries, all of which she attributed to falls. Why, Jonny wondered, did she not simply tell the truth, that her husband was a vicious bully who abused her? The only answer he could come up with was the money. He'd obtained warrants to look at the Pearces' bank accounts. Ray Pearce had twenty grand stashed away in a savings account. Given the poor trade at the Spinners Arms, where had that come from?

Jonny parked up and went into the pub. It was quiet as usual, with only three people in — a trio of old blokes playing dominoes at a table near the door. They didn't even look up as he walked to the bar.

Rita Pearce nodded at a table well away from them. "Ray's at football, but he won't be long. How's Andy?"

Jonny could tell that she'd been crying, her eyes were red and her face pale. "Was it you who alerted the emergency services?"

"Yes. I was terrified. I'd no idea what had happened to Andy. I'd gone to have a word and found him lying like that on the kitchen floor. He was still conscious and tried to speak to me. He'd been attacked in the sitting room but had dragged himself into the kitchen because his mobile was there. He whispered that I should take it."

"Did he ring anyone?"

"He didn't have the strength. I did as he wanted and brought the phone home." She reached behind the bar and picked up a plastic bag containing the mobile. "Andy thought it was important, so it might help you catch whoever attacked him."

"And he didn't say anything about who that might be?"

"No, he passed out."

"You probably saved his life," Jonny told her. "You know more about Andy than anyone. You're friends. I need you to speak to me, tell me what made him a target. Who would want to harm him like that?"

"I don't know, and that's the truth. We're close because he knows what a brute Ray is, and he's tried to help me over the years, but Andy doesn't tell me everything."

"If Andy knows how Ray treats you, could he have tackled him and come off worst? You said your husband was at the football, but are you sure?"

"Ray hits me, everyone round here knows that," she spat. "Yes, Andy wanted to sort Ray once and for all. He hates him. But Ray didn't see him as a threat, not with his hand being like it is. Since Andy's accident, I don't think the two have said a single word to each other." She turned away. "They used to be friends, always together, but all that ended about three years ago."

It wasn't lost on Jonny that that was round about the time Gavin Wellburn was killed. He had to ask himself if either man could have been involved.

"Ray has a lot of money in a savings account. D'you know where it came from?"

"He told me it came from the sale of his parents' house after they died. I never questioned him about it. I was just pleased we had a nest egg if needed."

"And he's never fancied moving away from here, or even giving the pub a facelift?"

"Ray reckons doing the place up would be a waste of money. As for moving, I've always said no. At least round here I've got people I trust and who know the score — my barmaid, for one."

"You could always leave him," Jonny suggested.

"He'd find me, he's always said so. No, it's better this way. I do know how to handle Ray."

"If you need help at any time, Rita, give us a ring. Thanks for the mobile. Our tech people will look at it. Chances are it'll give us something we can use."

* * *

Rachel's head was spinning. Jed's news was bad enough, add to that what the stranger had told her and she was doubly confused. Jed was a problem she could do something about. A word with Alan might solve things, but if not, she'd have to persuade Jed what a bad idea it was. But Rachel couldn't make sense of what she'd just been told about her parents. They'd died as the result of a tragic car crash, confirmed by the police at the time and later by the coroner at the inquest. It was something Rachel had put behind her for the sake of her sanity. The last thing she needed was their deaths being dragged up and becoming a mystery.

There was no way Rachel felt able to drive home, so she took a taxi to Elwyn's. Rachel desperately needed a sympathetic ear and sound advice. Elwyn could be hard at times, dish out what she didn't want to hear, but he was her friend and she needed to talk.

It was late. With luck the others would have left by now. She couldn't share this with the rest of the team. It was far too personal and raw.

Elwyn's sister, Ffion, opened the door and ushered her in. "Here I am, playing hostess again for my brother. Just as well I only live up the road. There's food left," she said. "Elwyn's had too much wine, foolish man. It goes straight to his head, always has. So, don't take too much notice of him."

Rachel found the soft lilt of her Welsh accent soothing. Elwyn was lucky. The brother and sister had always been close, and she envied them that. Rachel was an only child and apart from her children and one ex-husband — and not counting Jed — she had no one else in the world.

"I'm not hungry, Ffion. I just need a word with Elwyn."

Rachel went through to the sitting room. All her team had gone, and the only people left were neighbours.

One of them grinned. "This your young lady?"

"This is my boss," Elwyn corrected with a silly grin. "So mind your tongue or she'll chew me up in the morning."

"Can I have a word?" Rachel asked him.

"Is it the case?"

"No, it's personal." Rachel flopped down on to the nearest chair and kicked off her shoes.

Elwyn rounded up the neighbours. "Come on, you lot, much as I've enjoyed your company, me and the boss still have work to do."

"I'll make a drink," Ffion offered. "Hot chocolate?"

Ffion hadn't offered the usual glass of wine. That meant Elwyn hadn't been able to resist. Rachel smiled at her. "You know, don't you?"

"Elwyn made me promise not to say a word to anyone about the baby, and I haven't. You know what he's like, excited as a child about the news. I'll make your drink and get off home."

Once everyone had gone, Elwyn sat on the sofa opposite her. He looked concerned. "You don't look right, Rachel. Has something happened?"

"I've had a weird night," she said. "First with Jed and then . . ."

"You look done in. D'you want to stay here? I've got a spare room."

"Would you mind? I haven't the energy to drive home."

Ffion returned with Rachel's drink. "I'm off home now." She looked at Elwyn. "I might catch you in the morning before you leave."

"Ready to talk now?" Elwyn asked once they were alone.

"Would you believe that my new neighbour is Jed?" Elwyn's mouth dropped open. "Alan sold to him. He must have known what he was doing, he's seen Jed before, and I bet Mia has said stuff that made it sound like a good idea."

"In many ways it might be beneficial," he said. "You're having his baby — he'll be on hand to help."

"A sort of swap Alan for Jed scenario? I can't see that working. Jed's not the hands-on type around babies."

"How d'you know? You've never seen him in action. From what I know about your past, you've never given him the chance. You were with Alan when you had both girls. But if it's really bothering you, why not have a word with Alan, ask him not to go ahead with the sale to Jed."

"It's not just the Jed problem — and that has the potential to be a biggie, make no mistake. Something odd happened when I left the restaurant, and in many respects, it shook me up even more than Jed's news. A young man approached me outside the restaurant and started to talk about my parents. He said that the car crash in which they were killed wasn't an accident. I don't know what to make of it. It really spooked me, Elwyn."

"It'll have been a mistake," he said. "Has to be. Perhaps he thought you were someone else."

"No, he knew my name and my parents' names." She looked at him. "You don't think there could be anything in it? I saw nothing untoward in the police and forensics reports when I read them."

"Then forget it. He's probably some crank who read something in the paper and fancies making trouble."

Somehow Rachel didn't think so. He'd been telling the truth. She'd seen it in his eyes.

CHAPTER TWENTY-SEVEN

Saturday

"Thank you all for giving up your precious weekend break to be here. I know we've all got better things to do, but it can't be helped. We've got a lot to get through if we're to wrap this case up," Rachel said.

Rachel owed them. It was early on a Saturday morning and the whole team had turned up, even Stella. Both Amy and Jonny were supposed to have had this weekend off, and no doubt Elwyn could do with the time to sort out his new house.

"Andy Siddall is still in a coma. His doctors have said that they may try to bring him round today. But his evidence is crucial, we need to know who attacked him and why, so let's hope he pulls through." She looked at Jonny. "I've read your report on last night. Rita Pearce — speak to her again. The woman is still holding back. If we're to find out who assaulted Siddall, we need her to talk to us. I'm certain that there is some secret about that mill and what went on there that no one will talk about. And I don't just mean the murder of Gavin Wellburn." She looked at the latest notes on the incident board. "Looking at the paperwork from the bank, we see that both Ray Pearce and Andy Siddall had amounts of money deposited in their accounts, but it's not much."

"Do you think it's significant?" Amy asked.

"Until we know different, everything is significant, Amy."

"I'm having Siddall's mobile processed," Jonny said. "He told Rita it was important."

"Elwyn had been flicking through some papers. He looked up and caught Rachel's eye. "Sherwin's list, ma'am. I haven't had time to sort through it yet, it's been lying in my to-do pile. But I think we might have a problem."

"How so?"

"He's given us a number of alibis for the dates Healey reckons he was dealing. And in most instances the alibi is the same person, including for the night Jonny saw him in the mill yard with Jasmine Pearce, dishing out drugs to those youngsters."

Rachel folded her arms. What alibi could he possibly have that would contradict what Jonny had seen with his own eyes?

Elwyn looked around at the team. "Believe it not, his alibi is Millie Shawcross."

"He has to be joking! How can Millie Shawcross possibly know a loser like Sherwin?" Jonny exclaimed. "And I know what I saw. It was him, alright."

"We're not doubting you, Jonny," Rachel said. "But it will have to be checked out. Elwyn, you and me will speak to Millie. Stella, dig out her contact details, will you?" She looked at Amy. "Carry on going through Sherwin's list. Where the alibi isn't Millie, discount any that we suspect are in his pocket and arrange to see the rest."

While Rachel had been speaking to the team Stella had been busy on the phone. Once the team had been briefed, she called to Rachel, "Dr Fox would like a word when you're free."

Rachel went into her office to ring him back straight away. It was Saturday, so he'd be doing overtime for them. "Jason, what've you got for us?"

"We've taken a closer look at that tunnel and it is even more interesting than we thought. We've found a number of objects you should see."

"Want to give me a clue?"

"Can I suggest that you come down? Then I can show you."

"Okay, on our way."

"Elwyn!" she called. "We'll take a detour via Shawcross Mill. Jason's found something."

* * *

As he drove them out, Elwyn asked, "How are you this morning?"

"Much better. Ffion made me breakfast and stood over me while I ate it. I slept well, too. Thanks for putting me up. Last night was a strange one. My brain was busting with what Jed told me, and then there was the other thing."

"Do you intend to do anything about that?" Elwyn asked.

"No, it's history. Like you say, just some nutcase chancing his arm."

"Dare I ask what you intend to do about Jed?" Elwyn gave her a quick glance.

Rachel leaned back and closed her eyes. What to do about Jed, a perennial problem. It all looked so easy to those on the outside — Elwyn, for example. But how could she take up with Jed again? They weren't kids any more and they'd never been able to spend more than a few hours together without arguing.

Rachel wanted to shelve all thoughts of Jed, but Elwyn had asked, and he was right to do so. She couldn't ignore Jed or the baby for much longer, and it was doing her head in. "I've no idea what I'll do or when. These last weeks, I've banished all thoughts of the problem to some obscure corner of my mind. That can't continue — I've got a scan next week. But one thing I'm sure of, I'm not moving. That cottage is our home. The girls love it and have friends there, Mia's school, and a settled life."

"In that case, you'll have to accept that he's your new neighbour."

"Or I could persuade Alan not to sell."

"Rachel, you're not thinking about this logically. When the baby comes, Jed will be a help. It's his child too, or have you forgotten that?"

"Of course not, but it won't be that simple. Jed will want into my life. All of it. He'll want us to be a couple, and that's a huge commitment."

"It could be what you need. Jed isn't the pariah he once was. I mean,

even Kenton has accepted him."

"The problem is with me, not Jed. I'm not sure I want him around on a full-time basis. I did once, but I'm not the same person now. I value my independence — well, such as it is, given the kids. Jed has no idea about my life, the job, the hours or the stress. It drove Alan crazy when we were together."

"You don't have much choice, Rachel. Tell Jed and sort your life out."

Elwyn was right. She had to face this head on before it drove her mad. "Okay, I promise I'll sort it. I'll ask Jed round to the house and tell him."

"When?"

"I'm not sure. Soon."

CHAPTER TWENTY-EIGHT

At Shawcross Mill, access to the space below the cellar had been made easier by the installation of a set of temporary stairs with a handrail. But Rachel still had to tackle them with care. One slip could put paid to her pregnancy and, to her surprise, she found she didn't want that.

Rachel had been feeling ambivalent about the baby. Did she want it, or did she not? There was still plenty of time to decide. But now, apparently, she did want it, and very much so. The realisation made her smile. It lifted her spirits and gave her something exciting to look forward to. She'd been a fool to think otherwise. There were plenty of women who'd give their eyeteeth to be in her position.

When she got to the bottom of the steps, Rachel saw just how much work had been done to excavate the tunnel. It couldn't have been easy. Whoever had left Wellburn here had planned carefully, obviously never expecting him to be found.

"A little digging, clearing out the brick and earth that had fallen in and it's useable again," Jason told them. "Not that I've explored the entire length of the thing, it could lead anywhere. But according to the map on the wall up there, and the trajectory, it does go towards the Victorian brickyard like we discussed. The brickyard itself isn't there any more. Once the mill was built, the land was cleared and the Shawcross incumbent at the time built terraced houses on the site."

Rachel peered into blackness. "Any light?"

"Sorry, yes." Jason flicked a switch and the first few metres of the tunnel materialised in a bluish glow. "We found one or two things — this, for example." He held up a jewellery box. "It's plush velvet inside, shaped to take a ring. The name inside the lid is 'Tiffany,' but there's nothing in it." He grinned. "What's the betting that whatever it contained was expensive?"

Rachel looked at Elwyn. "I wonder what that means? Who would bring a box like that down here?"

"That's anybody's guess," Elwyn said.

"While you're puzzling that one out, try puzzling this one, too. Two supermarket trolleys. That's about it." Jason smiled.

"Well, it's certainly interesting, not that it makes much sense," said Rachel.

"The flotsam of many years finding its way down from above," Jason said. "Although I haven't found where it could have got in."

"If it was down to littering, you'd expect to see more stuff lying about, but there's nothing. In fact, once inside, beyond where the body was found, the tunnel is pretty clear," said Elwyn.

"It is now," Jason said. "But there is evidence that it was flooded and silted up at one time. Perhaps someone cleaned it up."

He was smiling, but that was a distinct possibility if the tunnel had been used to get in and out of the mill. It needed some thought. The Tiffany box could be important but then again, its presence down here might mean nothing at all.

"Thanks, Jason. Anything else, let me know," Rachel said.

Her head was buzzing with possibilities. Perhaps people had had access to that tunnel in the more recent past and, like Jason had said, used it as a shortcut. But where to and for what reason? "Is there any chance of finding out where it leads to?" she asked. "It might be important."

"Okay, I'll make it a priority, but it could take time. We have no idea what we'll find as we get further in."

She and Elwyn climbed back up the stairs.

"What went on down there, Elwyn? Any suggestions? I know shopping trolleys turn up everywhere, in the canal and the like, but inside that tunnel? It doesn't seem possible."

"We know Sherwin uses the mill for his dealing. The items could have come from that. Perhaps he used the tunnel as a way of getting in and out of the mill without being seen. The trolleys could have been used to shift the gear."

"You're forgetting one thing." She nudged him. "The tunnel wasn't accessible — those lads fell through the wooden floorboards."

"Sherwin could have got in from the other end and hidden the gear this end," Elwyn suggested.

"We'll ask him, but first we'll talk to Millie Shawcross."

* * *

Millie Shawcross lived in a flat in Heaton Norris, on the outskirts of Stockport. "According to Stella's research she shares the flat with a girlfriend," Elwyn said.

"Do we know if she's working?" Rachel asked.

"She helps her father manage Shawcross Estates, but it's the weekend so she should be at home," Elwyn said.

"She knows Jonny from university," Rachel told him. "Millie recognised him when we were at the house. But she was calling herself Millie Fenwick when he knew her. It was her mother's maiden name, apparently. I keep wondering why."

"Could be any reason," Elwyn said. "Perhaps Millie and her dad fell out about something. It was a nasty divorce. It was all in the papers at the time. His ex-wife took him to the cleaners."

"Do we know what broke them up?"

"No, and Stella can't find anything either. His ex now lives in South Manchester somewhere. But whatever the reason, Millie took her mother's side and changed her name. Obviously, she no longer wanted to be associated with the Shawcross family."

"Changed her mind since, though, hasn't she? She's working for her dad and they seem pretty close. No doubt she's set to inherit the lot one day."

CHAPTER TWENTY-NINE

Millie Shawcross recognised Rachel at once. "If this is Shawcross business you should speak to my dad," she told them. "I deal with the office stuff, so if it's about the mill I won't be much help." She led them into a large sitting room overlooking the back garden. "It's a great place, isn't it? Me and Janey have the entire ground floor. Rent's not bad either."

"Better than the Shawcross mansion?" Rachel asked. "You had all the space in the world there, and no doubt lived rent free."

"That's my business," Millie said. "But if you must know, it was hard living with my dad. He didn't give me any freedom and he watched my every move. I felt like a prisoner."

In a way, Rachel could understand his concern, particularly if Millie was mixing with the likes of Sherwin. His daughter was all Mathew Shawcross had left. He would be desperate to keep her safe. But on the other hand, he'd lost his wife for the very same reason.

Rachel got straight to the point. "Do you know Billie Sherwin?"

Millie looked from one detective to the other. Finally, she nodded. She looked nervous, unsure of what to say. She obviously knew it was a tricky question and was probably wondering how to respond.

"Yes," she admitted at last. He lives somewhere near the mill. Drinks at a bar in town — that's where I met him."

"Billy is in custody for a serious offence," Elwyn told her. "He's given you as an alibi. We admit to being confused, Millie. Sherwin has a reputation. He is implicated in drug dealing that was going on at the mill."

Millie turned aside, chewing on her bottom lip. "That has to be wrong. You've got him confused with someone else. It can't be Billy because I see him quite a lot around town. Like I said, we frequent the same bar and mix with the same crowd."

"What were you doing on Thursday night?" Rachel asked.

"The usual, drinking in the bars around Oxford Road," she said. "And before you ask, yes, Billy was with us. Me, Janey, Billy and some others. We were bar hopping and then we went to eat at a curry house in Fallowfield."

"What times, exactly?" asked Elwyn.

"From about six until just before midnight. I remember because me and Janey got the last bus home."

Millie Shawcross had tried to sound convincing, but Rachel was suspicious. The young woman was twitchy, nervous. She couldn't stand still for a start but kept pacing the floor. There was something wrong. She was lying. Jonny had been sure he'd heard Jasmine Pearce call Billy's name and Rachel had complete faith in the young DC. Now she was puzzled. Why would the young woman stand up for Sherwin like this?

"Does Billy often go out with you and your friends?" Rachel asked.

"Yes, most nights. There's a group of us. He stays here sometimes too. He's between places currently and relies on his friends for a place to sleep."

Elwyn shook his head. "That's not the Billy Sherwin we know. We've been told he's a drug dealer who ropes in young kids to do his dirty work for him."

Millie laughed. "Never in a million years! Not Beef! He's far too soft. Big as he is, he would never mix with the sort of people you meet dealing. I don't know who's been feeding you this rubbish, but it's wrong."

"It was one of my own officers witnessed the incident on Thursday night," Rachel said. "Don't lie to me, Millie. I will get the truth and I won't take kindly to you lying to us."

"Billy's okay. You can take my word for it."

"What's his relationship with Jasmine Pearce?" Elwyn asked.

"Friends, I expect. Beef is friends with everyone around where she lives."

"He rarely sets foot in the Spinners Arms, which Jasmine lives above. How do you square that one?"

"Bad pint? Had words with that idiot landlord, her father? Who knows? Why not just ask him?"

Millie had her back to them and was staring out of the window at the garden. Rachel put a hand on her shoulder. "Why are you protecting him, Millie? Does he have some sort of hold over you? If he does, we can help." It was the only thing Rachel could think of. "I've interviewed Sherwin. He's nasty, brutal, the last person I'd imagine you'd be involved with."

Millie shrugged her hand away. "You people think you're clever but you're not. Far from it. You're stupid, all of you. You know nothing about Beef, the mill or anything else. Get out and leave me alone. I'm not saying anything else."

Millie went silent. For some reason she was shielding Sherwin, and no amount of reasoning with her was going to change her mind.

Outside on the street, Rachel looked up at the house. "She's lying, Elwyn. Millie Shawcross is like the rest of them, holding something back. What, I can only guess at, but my instincts tell me there's some secret involving that mill, something bad, and that's why no one will say anything."

Elwyn nodded. "I'll see if I can find anything that links Sherwin with the Shawcross family. You never know."

"In the meantime, much as it grates, we'll have to let him go. Sherwin's alibi holds up," Rachel said. She cursed softly under her breath. "I hate days like this, Elwyn. Everything goes wrong and we go around and around in circles."

While they were on their way back to the station, Rachel's mobile rang, a number she didn't recognise.

She heard a woman's voice. "Hello, DCI King. I'm DCI Nell Hennessey from Tameside Serious Crime Squad. We haven't met before, but I wonder if you've got time for a quick word."

Rachel didn't recognise the name and as far as she was aware, East Manchester had no current dealings with Tameside. "I'm in the middle of a tricky case at the moment. Can it wait a few days?"

"Fair enough. Bad habit of mine, dropping stuff on people. How about I come to your station on Monday next week?"

"Fine. Are you going to give me a clue as to what this is about?"

"I'd rather wait until we meet, Rachel, if that's okay."

"Can't say I'm not curious, but I'll have to contain myself, I guess. See you Monday. Shall we say about lunch-time? We could go and get something to eat."

"Good idea. My shout."

Call ended, Rachel turned to Elwyn. "That was a strange one. What d'you reckon a DCI from Tameside wants with me? She's coming over for lunch next Monday."

"Advice, information, could be anything," Elwyn said.

"Everything work-related is on the system. All she has to do is look it up."

"No need to stress, Rachel, you'll find out soon enough. You've got quite enough going on at the moment."

He was right — the case for one, and then there was the tricky problem of her personal life. But at least she now knew what to do about the baby. She smiled to herself, hugging her belly. A boy would be nice, for a change.

CHAPTER THIRTY

Billy Sherwin was marched into the interview room flanked by two uniformed officers. He didn't look happy.

"Bloody cells aren't made for a bloke my size. Bed was too small, didn't sleep a wink, and the food's crap," Sherwin said.

"Tell me about your relationship with Millie Shawcross," Rachel said.

"Nowt much to tell. She's a mate, I hang around with her and some others."

"You're lying, Billie," Rachel said. "She's not your mate. I mean, why would a girl like her bother with the likes of you?"

"Mate or not, she's given me an alibi." He smiled smugly. "So, give me the good news. Tell me I can go."

Rachel gritted her teeth. This was all wrong, but regulations were regulations. What else could she do? She nodded at the uniforms. "He's free to go. Take him to the front desk and make sure he gets all his belongings."

Once Sherwin was out of the room, Rachel banged her fist on the table. "Millie's not stupid, she must know he's an evil bastard! But why is she lying to us? What hold does he have over her? There has to be something, Elwyn."

"Something big, otherwise why not speak out against him? But think, Rachel. The dealing is one thing, but is he our killer?" Elwyn said.

"Something happened in that mill three years ago, and it involved Wellburn, Sherwin, possibly Siddall and Rita's husband. That's why none of them will speak to us, they're all covering for each other."

"Nice theory, but that's all it is, Rachel. And unless one of them speaks to us, that's the way it will stay."

"Okay, who's the weak link? Which one of them will crack first and help us, Elwyn? My money is on Rita Pearce."

"I think you're right. It would help to know who they're all so scared of. We've met a wall of silence since the beginning and that's not natural. We get vague answers to our questions, no one remembers anything . . . Rita Pearce runs the boozer on that street, for pity's sake, she must know more than she's told us."

"Sherwin," Rachel stated. "Stands to reason, the man's a thug. Given what happened to Siddall, she might be willing to talk now. We'll interview her again, but first let's get an up-to-date prognosis on Siddall."

* * *

Elwyn phoned the hospital and it was good news. Andy Siddall had been brought out of the induced coma. He was doing well and was out of danger. Elwyn left word that they would be round to interview him later in the day. With luck, he'd be able to identify his assailant and get them a step nearer to solving this case.

"Stella," he said, sitting down beside her. "I want you to do something for me, but quietly. Don't let the boss know."

She smiled. "You've got me curious."

"Get hold of the CCTV from Deansgate for last night, say nine thirty to ten. Particularly around the Imperial restaurant."

"What am I looking for?" she asked.

"Rachel. She was there last night, and a young man stopped her outside on the pavement. He spoke to her for several minutes, so the camera should have picked them up."

"You're after an identity for him?"

"If possible. Rachel didn't know who he was."

Stella nodded. "If I get anything, I'll text you the clip."

Rachel had enough on her plate without any added worry. A little research on her behalf would do no harm. Elwyn knew that Rachel's parents had died five years ago, not long after she'd divorced Alan. A quick search and he found the record on the system. It appeared to be straightforward enough — a wet night, poor visibility, and a camera they'd passed a couple of miles before the accident had them speeding. It was presumed that Rachel's father had lost control on a sharp bend and run full speed into a small wooded area at the side of the road. The report said there was no CCTV where the accident happened. The road was rural, but busy. All they had to go on was footage from the camera that had caught them speeding. Later, when he had time, he'd take a closer look at that.

CHAPTER THIRTY-ONE

Andy Siddall lay propped up on pillows with an oxygen mask on his face. Rachel and Elwyn entered the room and sat down by the bed.

He'd been battered about the head. His eyes were black and he had a gash down his right cheek. "You're a lucky man," Rachel said. "The person who did this left you for dead. Who was it, Andy? Who have you upset so badly that they did this you? You must have seen him."

Siddall shook his head and pulled away the mask so he could speak. "Yes, I saw him," he croaked, "but I've no idea who he was."

Beaten and shot, left for dead and he still wouldn't speak. What was wrong with these people? "A description, then. Was he young? Tall? How was he dressed?" Rachel asked.

Siddall turned pale. Was the memory too fresh? Too much too soon? Should they be pushing him like this when he'd taken a knock to the head and lost a lot of blood? Rachel was frustrated but she'd have to back off.

"Are you up to telling us what happened?" Elwyn asked gently, catching Rachel's eye. "We want to apprehend who-ever did this to you, but we can't do that without your help."

125

Elwyn was trying the softer approach. Rachel hoped it would work.

Siddall nodded. "He surprised me. The doorbell rang. The dog went wild, barking his head off, so I put him outside in the back yard before I went to see who it was. I only opened the door a touch, but the bloke barged in and started lashing out. I didn't see much of him, only his shape and clothing. He was dressed in black with a balaclava pulled down over his face. He followed me into the kitchen and started shooting. He chased me all around the bloody house, lashing out with that gun of his. He caught my face with the butt, hence the cut. I might have got out, but I tripped over a mat in the hall. I was lying flat out on my belly when he shot me. I was terrified, thought I might die. I'd no idea how bad it was. That's about it. That's all I can remember."

"Did no one come to help you, a neighbour, perhaps?"

"The gun had a silencer, I doubt they heard."

"You've done pretty well," Elwyn said. "Were you unconscious?"

"I think so. When I fell in the hall, I knocked my head on the old sideboard I keep in there. But I came to pretty quick. I knew my mobile was in the kitchen, so I dragged myself in there to get a hold of it and call for help. I think that's when I passed out again."

"Did you notice a car on the street?" Rachel asked.

"Couldn't say. The neighbours might have seen something, but after I was shot, he legged it out the door. Once I got to the kitchen, I couldn't move again. I think I must have been bleeding out."

"Rita saved your life. You're lucky she turned up when she did. She gave you first aid and then rang for an ambulance. Did you know she was coming?" Rachel asked.

He looked at them rather sheepishly. "No, but she visits sometimes when she wants to talk. Me and Rita — it's not what you think. She did have someone once, apart from Ray. They were very fond of each other and would have made a go of it if things had been different. He was the one man she'd have risked leaving that brute for."

"Can you give me a name?" Rachel asked.

"No, I can't, but it's not me. I'm there for her because she needs someone in her corner. Poor woman gets nowt but abuse from that husband of hers, and her daughter isn't much help. Whenever Rita gets down, needs a shoulder, you know, she comes to me."

"Does her husband know about your relationship?" Rachel asked.

"No, I don't think so. What are you getting at?"

"That it might've been him who attacked you. Ray Pearce is a jealous bully. He wouldn't take kindly to anyone seeing his wife on a regular basis."

"It wasn't him. Too nimble on his feet," Andy said. "Ray's got dodgy knees."

"Well, whoever did this to you might try again. He'll know pretty soon that you're still alive. That bullet was meant to kill you. It wasn't just a warning," Rachel said. "Can you think of a reason why anyone would want you dead, Andy? We need the truth. We keep asking questions but get nowhere. No one will speak to us, and we can't work out what they're all so scared of."

Siddall looked away. Rachel could see from the expression on his face that her words had hit the mark. "It's not that easy. I talk to you and I'm dead for sure. Whatever you might think, this could be just a warning, so leave me in peace. I'm not saying another word."

"I hope you're right, Andy," Elwyn said, "about it being a warning. If it's not, you've just given up any chance you had of saving yourself."

"Don't push it, copper! You have no idea what we're up against."

Rachel looked at him. What did he mean? "Then tell us, Andy. Tell us what you're so afraid of and we'll help you."

"Get lost. I daren't say anything more."

"We'll leave a guard on the door," Rachel said. "That'll keep you safe while you're here, but once you get home, you're on your own again."

Siddall held up his damaged hand. "I've been up against it before. They didn't win back then, either."

"I thought that was an accident at work," Elwyn said.

"It happened while I was working, yes, but it was no accident. Now, get out. I've said too much already."

"Are you telling us someone deliberately assaulted you?" Rachel asked. "If so, I don't understand why you remained silent about it."

"You coppers have no idea. I've said all I'm going to on the matter, now go and leave me in peace."

The two of them took the stairs in silence. Rachel was trying to make sense of what Siddall had said. "His hand, Elwyn. Not an accident, so who would do that to him, and why?"

"Siddall's been injured twice now. To me, that smacks of someone trying to ensure he keeps quiet. I'll lay odds he knows who killed Wellburn."

"Siddall, Wellburn and who else?" Rachel thought for a moment. "We'll have another word with Rita. She has to talk to us, Elwyn."

"Don't forget Mathew Shawcross," Elwyn said. "We still need to speak to him about that tunnel. He might know something that can help us."

"I wonder if he knows the people his daughter mixes with. He can't approve of Sherwin, surely."

"I think she was lying," Elwyn said. "A girl like her doesn't go around with a villain like Sherwin. She's another one that's terrified of telling the truth."

CHAPTER THIRTY-TWO

Rita Pearce didn't seem surprised to see the two detectives. She nodded to a window table, indicating they should sit down while she finished serving a couple at the bar. There were at least a dozen other people at the Spinners Arms. Rachel had never seen the place so busy.

"We serve food Saturday lunchtimes," Rita said. "It's about the only time we do any trade. To be honest, I don't know why we stay on. I've wanted to move out for a long time, but Ray won't hear of it. He's convinced that one day trade will go back to what it was, and we'll be quids in again. But he's wrong. This place, the entire area, has had it. The whole lot wants tearing down and redeveloping."

"The pub's not profitable, then?" Elwyn asked.

"No. We'll do alright today, but that's about it."

Rachel smiled at her. "You did well, saving Andy like that, Rita. Without your help he would certainly have died. The bullet wound had severed an artery and the blood loss could have been catastrophic."

"I was working on instinct. I've got no training, but I knew putting pressure on it should stem the flow. The only thing I could get my hands on was the cushion. I pressed it to the wound and lay him on top of it."

"You arrived pretty promptly after the attack. You knew how bad he was, but you didn't wait with him. Why, Rita?" asked Rachel.

"I was terrified that Ray would find out. He's a vicious bastard. He'd have laid into both me and Andy if he thought we were more than friends."

"Did you see anyone, catch sight of a car as you left? Perhaps someone in a hurry to leave the area?" Elwyn asked.

"There was one, a black Ford, an old one that looked as if it'd been souped up. You know, a spoiler on the back and fancy stripes down the sides. It sped out of the crescent at a fair lick. I'd just got off the bus when it went past me. Luckily, no one was coming the other way."

"Did you get a registration number?" asked Elwyn.

Rita shook her head. "I'd no idea then that it was important. Look, I've got to get on. This lot want serving and there's only me on."

"We believe Andy knows who attacked him, but he won't say. What's your take on it, Rita?" Rachel asked her. "Who is he afraid of? Billy Sherwin, perhaps?"

Rita looked mildly amused. "Is that what you think?"

"We don't know what to think, but we do know Sherwin is selling drugs out of that mill across the road, and that people are so afraid of the man that they're prepared to lie for him, even his girlfriend Millie Shawcross."

"Get on the wrong side of him and Sherwin's a nasty bugger. He's responsible for putting several people in hospital. But you're wrong about the Shawcross girl. She's not involved with Sherwin. She's going out with a lad called Damon Brooke, has been for a while. And it wasn't Sherwin had a go at Andy either."

"Even if they're not involved, Sherwin and Millie have friends in common."

Rita shook her head. "I doubt it. She's a Shawcross. They're worlds apart. You must have it wrong."

* * *

But Millie Shawcross had told them to their faces that Sherwin was a friend. Why would she lie for him if that weren't so? Rachel was losing patience. No one involved with any aspect of this case would tell her the truth.

"Another word with Millie? Or do we speak to her father?" Elwyn asked once they were back in the car.

"I'm trying to work out why she'd tell us a blatant lie. The only thing that makes any sense is that Sherwin has some sort of hold over her."

"Or over the boyfriend. I'll speak to Stella, get her to find out about this Damon Brooke. He could be an addict. If he is, and Sherwin is his dealer, that's hold enough."

Elwyn finished his call to Stella just as Rachel's mobile rang. It was Amy. She put her on speaker.

"I'm in Ardwick, ma'am. We got called out to a shooting. It's Billy Sherwin. He's been murdered."

Rachel wondered what Sherwin was doing at Ardwick. "Check if he's been living there," she said. Millie had mentioned he'd been staying with friends, she remembered.

After weighing everything up, Rachel decided that drugs were at the bottom of what was going on, Sherwin was surely at the head of the operation. He was the main man everyone was terrified of crossing. But was she right? He'd just been shot, so who had been brave enough to take him on?

"That sorts out where we're going next. Someone's put paid to Sherwin's reign of terror their own way."

* * *

While Elwyn drove, Rachel tried to make sense of it. Sherwin had to have enemies, he was a dealer, but why would they kill him now? And was his murder in any way connected to what had happened to Siddall?

The entire fourth floor of the tower block had been cordoned off and forensics had started their search for evidence. They had their work cut out — the ground was littered with rubbish. Trying to sort out what was relevant would be difficult.

"Bullet to the chest, straight through the heart. Quick and effective," Colin Butterfield told them when they arrived.

Putting on the gloves and overshoes handed to them, Rachel and Elwyn went inside the flat. The place was a mess. The only furniture was a battered sofa covered in bits of food, and a table littered with empty lager cans. Sherwin was lying face down on a mat, a pool of blood spreading out from beneath his body.

"Who called it in?" Rachel asked.

"A neighbour. He was killed within the last hour," Jude said. "There's no sign of a break-in, so perhaps he knew his killer. He put up a fight, too, he's got grazed knuckles. There's every possibility that I'll get DNA from the wounds."

"Thanks, Jude. Meanwhile, we'll get uniform to go door to door. Given that he was shot, someone must have heard something."

Jude smiled wryly. "Round here? Don't count on it. People close their ears and turn a blind eye. Besides, there are precious few tenants left. This block is scheduled for demolition. In the meantime, it's being used to house some of Manchester's rough sleepers. People who don't usually like talking to us."

Among the homeless using this place there'd be any number of users — that'd be why Sherwin was here. He'd have a constant flow of customers and their cash.

"We had him in custody, Jude. He gave us an alibi that held up, so we had no choice but to let him go just a few hours ago."

"Don't beat yourself up, Rachel. He was clever. He knew all the angles and wielded a lot of power. He was a dealer big-time, there's a small fortune in crack cocaine in those bags on the table over there, and a whole lot of cash in that drawer."

"Not robbery, then. Whoever did this wasn't interested in the drugs or the cash. That could narrow it down."

"To what?" asked Elwyn.

"Retribution," Rachel said. "Someone who thought he was too dangerous to be allowed to live."

CHAPTER THIRTY-THREE

Rachel and Elwyn headed back to Heaton Norris for another chat with Millie Shawcross. Sherwin was dead, so there was no need for her to hold back on the truth any more. They found the young woman in a state, she had obviously been crying.

"It's Damon," she said. "He's been hurt."

"Damon Brooke, your boyfriend?" asked Elwyn. "You didn't mention him earlier when we were here. And I don't think you were being entirely truthful when you gave Billy Sherwin that alibi."

She shook her head. "I'm sorry, alright! But I had no choice. I'm a bloody fool. I walk away from one control freak straight into the arms of another. Sherwin's and me are over but he's a force you can't ignore. He tells you to do something, you do it. If I hadn't said those things, given him the alibi, he'd have hurt Damon."

"Where is Damon?" Rachel asked.

She nodded to the sitting room. "He arrived half an hour ago. He won't say what happened, or who attacked him, but he's got a cut face and a black eye."

Rachel wondered if he'd been to the flat where they found Sherwin. Had the pair argued, and Brooke shot him?

Before going to talk to Brooke, she went into the hallway and rang Stella.

"Do you have anything on Brooke yet?" Rachel queried.

"He's been arrested twice for possession. Last month he tried rehab, but only stuck it out for a day."

"An addict, then. Thanks, Stella."

But if Brooke had gone to Sherwin to buy drugs, why not take what was on the table?

"Where have you been, Damon?" Rachel asked him. "Who did this to you?"

His face was bruised. He'd taken quite a pasting. Whoever had hit him hadn't held back.

"I don't know who it was. I was attacked out in the street," Damon said.

"Was it in Ardwick?" asked Rachel

Damon shook his head. "I've never been near the place."

"What did he look like, this person who attacked you?" asked Elwyn.

"He was some bloke dressed in black, tall, and wearing a balaclava over his head and face."

That was how Siddall had described the man who'd attacked him.

"You're lying, Damon. You were in Ardwick to buy drugs off Sherwin."

"No! I said, I've never been there."

"That's a lie," Rachel said. "He was your dealer. The forensics crew are there now. What's the betting they find your prints all over Billy Sherwin's flat? Why not save us all a lot of trouble and tell the truth?"

Millie nudged him. "Tell them, Damon. They'll just find out anyway, and then it'll be worse."

"Okay. I knocked at Sherwin's door and this bloke came crashing out. He didn't say a word, just thumped me in the face and knocked me over. Then he dragged me to the staircase and shoved me, and I fell down half a dozen steps or so. I called out but he was gone in seconds. When I got my breath back, I went inside to find out what had happened and found Sherwin dead."

"Did you touch anything, try to help him?"

"No. I didn't know what to do. I ran out and knocked on the flat next door. She rang you lot."

Rachel looked at Millie. "What you told us earlier. Am I to take it that the whole lot was a pack of lies?"

"Sherwin said he'd do Damon serious harm if I didn't give him an alibi. He said he could make things awkward for my dad, too."

That was an odd thing to say. This case was complex enough, but so far Mathew Shawcross hadn't been mentioned. "Awkward in what way, Millie? What could Sherwin possibly have over your dad?"

"He didn't say, just that he knew things that my dad wouldn't want to get out."

"We've looked at Sherwin's history. We know he was a dealer but can find no trace of the money he must have made."

"It's in a bank account in another name," Millie said. "Sherwin had several of them, so nothing could be traced back to him."

"Do you know any of the names he used?"

"There's a notebook somewhere in that flat. The details are all in there."

"You've been very foolish, Millie," Elwyn said. "You should have told us the truth from the start. Is there anything else that you're keeping from us?"

"No. All this has happened because Damon needs that filthy stuff, and Sherwin played on that. He threatened to tell my dad and stop Damon's supply if I refused to help him."

"What d'you think he had on your dad, Millie?"

"It was probably all talk. Sherwin lied all the time. You never knew whether he was telling the truth or not."

Nonetheless, Rachel would give it some consideration. Mathew Shawcross had a strong motive for harming

Sherwin — he was using his daughter, involving her in his dirty business.

"How long had Sherwin been dealing at the mill?" Rachel asked them.

"No more than a couple of years," Millie said.

* * *

After two PCs took Millie and her boyfriend to the station so they could give their statements, Rachel turned to Elwyn. "We'll have to speak to Shawcross," she said. "About his daughter, but also that tunnel."

Elwyn grimaced. "We won't be popular, having just hauled his daughter in."

"It's hardly that. Millie is just giving us her side of things. Granted, she lied about Sherwin, but she was under duress. It's Brooke that bothers me. He did have a motive for killing Sherwin. We need to trace his movements in the time leading up to the shooting."

Elwyn was checking his phone. "It's getting late and you haven't eaten all day."

"Keeping tabs on me, eh?" She smiled. "We'll go back to the station and then get off home."

"Wonder if your new neighbour's taken up residence yet."

The idea made her feel sick. "Oh, please! I'm not ready for him yet. I'm still hoping to find a way to put him off."

"It's Sunday tomorrow. Work as usual, is it?"

"Both Jonny and Amy were supposed to be off this weekend. I feel like an ogre dragging them into work."

"Leave it optional. Perhaps they can do half a day each. But you can count on me, I'll be there, slogging away. It might be an idea for you to have a lie-in, get some proper rest."

He was trying to be kind, but how could she take time off? Come Monday morning, Kenton would be at her office door, and she still didn't have a killer for Gavin Wellburn.

CHAPTER THIRTY-FOUR

Sunday

Rachel slept late. She hadn't meant to, but she was exhausted. And she woke up feeling nauseous. She groaned. She'd hoped the morning sickness wouldn't strike this time. When she'd been pregnant with the other two it had gone on for weeks. With Megan it had laid her so low she'd been unable to work.

She grabbed her mobile from the bedside table. "Elwyn," she said. "I can't make it today. I'm not skiving, honestly, I'm not so good."

"Don't worry, Rachel, I understand," Elwyn said.

But would the others? "Amy and Jonny? They won't understand."

"I'll sort them. They're both in and hard at it."

That made Rachel feel even worse. "Whatever you tell them, Elwyn, make it sound good. They'll think I'm using my rank, having the day off while they're working and I'm not. I feel such a wimp."

"I'll tell them something convincing — looking at forensic evidence at the labs, checking statements, don't worry. By the way, Brooke has an alibi. He was in the entrance to the block helping an elderly woman up the stairs with her shopping. They were together when they heard the shot."

"Not him, then." She sighed. "That would have been far too easy."

"I'll see you tomorrow, Rachel. Enjoy your day."

Rachel pulled on a dressing gown and went downstairs to be met by Megan.

"Heavy night, Mum? You certainly look as if you had a good time."

"No, love, far more mundane than that. It's something I ate."

"That bloke's next door talking to Dad. You kept that secret, didn't you? He's an old flame of yours, I hear. Very handy that's going to be, having him as a neighbour."

Rachel shook her head. Megan couldn't be more wrong, but she didn't have the energy to explain.

"I'm off to Sophie's. We're going to work out stuff for when I move in. She's asked for next month's rent up front. What d'you think?"

"What did you expect? Paying your way is part of the deal."

"It's five hundred quid, Mum, and I don't have a bean."

"You want a loan?"

"Think of it as a donation!" Megan grinned. "Dad's giving me some dosh for furniture, so it's only fair that you chip in. Think how good it'll be to have me out of the way. You and that old boyfriend of yours can get all cosy without me spying on the pair of you. I'm off now, I'll leave you to think about it."

Rachel poured herself some juice from the fridge, went into the sitting room and peered out through the window. Jed's car was parked outside. That meant he was at Alan's. What were they talking about? She felt the butterflies in her stomach. She could only hope that it was about the house sale and she hadn't been the hot topic. The idea that Alan and Jed were talking about her was weird enough without the worry that Jed would say something out of turn. Could she trust him? Jed was a law unto himself, and now that Alan was moving out and he was moving in, he'd see no reason to watch his tongue.

She saw Alan's car pull away, followed by a knock on her front door.

Damn! Rachel didn't want this, and to top it all, she looked a right sight. At least with Megan out and Mia having stayed over at her best friend Ella's the night before, she was alone. Just as well. She didn't want the kids listening in to her conversation with Jed.

"What d'you want?" she said.

He thrust a bouquet of roses towards her and his face fell. "I don't expect much from you, Rachel, but I am trying very hard. Have these. I chose them specially."

"You're forcing your way into my life and I don't like it. I wish you'd just leave me alone."

"You don't mean that." Rachel saw the quizzical look. "What's up? You look a bit rough. Heavy night? Hit the town with your team, did you?"

"No, I bloody well did not. You'd better come in." It had started to rain — she couldn't leave him on the doorstep. She stood aside and gestured for him to follow her into the sitting room. "Are you still going ahead with next door?"

"Yes, I've got my legal team working hard to get everything sorted as fast as possible. I've paid a hefty deposit, the rest to follow on completion. I'm not waiting, I'm buying this house. It's a cash sale and I've signed a document drawn up by my solicitor to assure Alan that I will not pull out. That way he can go ahead with his plans in the meantime. I haven't haggled over price and will take the place as it is. Like it or not, Rachel, we'll be neighbours soon, so you'd better get used to the idea."

He was right. Short of moving herself, there was nothing she could do. Alan was thrilled to bits at having found a buyer so quickly and to be starting a new life with Belinda. No way could she spoil that for him.

Jed had made himself comfortable on her sofa and was watching her. "Something's wrong. You're not the same."

"Rubbish, it's early and I've just got up. I've not even brushed my hair."

"No, that's not it, there's something else."

"You! That's what's wrong with me." She folded her arms, pacing the floor. "You've done it again, wheedled your way back into my life. I'm sick of it."

"I can do without a mouthful, Rachel. I've not come here to argue. All I want is to see more of Mia. Surely you can understand that. I'm Mia's father, and I've already missed out on so many precious years. And I want to see more of you, too, if you'll let me."

His words struck home. Rachel felt a real pang of guilt. She had known that Mia was Jed's since she was an infant but had said nothing all these years.

"I mean it, Rachel. I should have told you I was buying the cottage, but I wanted it to be a surprise. You're free now, and so am I. There's no reason why we can't try to get on. Even better, rekindle our relationship. I still love you, in case you didn't know."

Rachel felt the tears well up in her eyes. She couldn't do this, she couldn't keep the truth from him a second time. He deserved to know.

"I'm pregnant," she whispered, avoiding his gaze. "With your baby. Malaga, remember?"

The silence that followed seemed endless. Finally, Rachel said, "Say something, please. Even if it's that you hate me."

"Of course I don't hate you. I love you, I always have. You're sure about the baby?"

"Positive. That's why I look so rough. I feel wretched most mornings."

"Another child. That's truly wonderful news." He smiled. "I'll get to see this one grow up."

"Oh, you'll do more than that, Jed McAteer, you're in on a fifty-fifty basis. The crying, the nappies, the sleepless nights, the bloody lot."

CHAPTER THIRTY-FIVE

Monday

On Monday morning, Elwyn collared Rachel on the stairs as she was on her way to the incident room. "You're late and you've got a visitor — Nell Hennessey. She's been here since eight. I've given her a coffee and stuck her in the soft interview room."

The DCI from Tameside! What with the events of the weekend, Rachel had forgotten about her.

"I might be late but she's early. Lunch, she said! I'll dump my stuff and see what she wants. Anything from forensics come in?" Rachel asked.

"Message from Jason. He wants you to ring him."

"I'll deal with my visitor first," she said.

DCI Nell Hennessey wasn't what Rachel had expected. She was older, for a start, about fifty. Her dark hair had flecks of grey. It was chin-length with no fringe and a slight wave, and she kept brushing it aside while she talked. There was no trace of make-up on her face. Her clothes were smart — a trouser suit with a white shirt — but her coat looked a couple of sizes too big.

"Rachel?" She stood up, smiled and held out a hand. "I'm Nell. Sorry to arrive so early, but I need your input on a case I'm investigating."

"That's okay. I'm sorry I was late in. It was panic stations at home this morning."

"You have a family? Kids?"

"Yes, and they're a demanding bunch."

"You're luck. There's only me and Dee, my mother, at home, and Betty, of course, our dog. Dee looks after the house and I do the work stuff. It suits us." She shrugged.

Referring to her mother by her first name, how very progressive. There was probably a story there, but there was no time now, Rachel had to get on. Jason wanted to talk to her and that meant he must have news. "How can I help?"

"I'd like you to look at something." Nell busied herself fishing around in the voluminous pockets of her coat for a few moments. "Sorry, Rachel, I was certain I'd brought it with me. You must think me a right disorganised mare. Which I am, by the way, but not usually with something so important."

Despite the name, which Rachel took to be Scottish, Nell Hennessey had a broad Northern accent. She was obviously a plain-speaking woman with no edge to her. Rachel recognised the type — said what she thought and always found a way of getting what she wanted.

"Found it," she said at last, producing her mobile. "Right, take a good look at the image and tell me if you've seen this young man before."

Rachel was stunned. It was the bloke from the night she'd eaten with Jed at the restaurant on Deansgate. The one with the fancy trainers who'd said her parents' death wasn't an accident. "Yes," she said. "I've seen him once."

"Did he speak to you?"

"Yes. He told me something very strange. I still don't know what to make of it."

"About your parents?"

Rachel handed the mobile back to her. "How d'you know that?"

"Because I'm familiar with how these people operate. He told you their death wasn't an accident?"

Rachel nodded. This was surreal. That young man had told her about a very personal event from the past that she'd buried and didn't like to think about. She'd no idea what it had to do with this oddball detective from a neighbouring force.

"It *was* an accident," Rachel told her. "My dad was speeding. It was a wet night and he took a bend too fast and crashed into some trees. Both my parents were killed outright. There were post-mortems, an inquest. No way was there a mistake."

"That young man is running a scam. He's approached other people with a similar story. Best thing is to take no notice of anything he told you." Nell smiled. "I appreciate you seeing me.

"What is he after, apart from upsetting folk?"

"He is just one aspect of a complex case my team are currently knee-deep in. Don't worry, Rachel, if anything comes out of it that you need to know, I'll be in touch."

Nell Hennessey was giving nothing away and Rachel was left feeling cheated. If there was a mystery surrounding her parents and how they'd died, she wanted to know about it.

* * *

"You alright?" Elwyn asked.

Rachel joined him and the others in the incident room. "Not here," she whispered.

"Jude wants us at the lab, and then Jason's asked if we can go and see him at the mill."

"Sounds like a day out. I'll get my stuff."

"You're looking a bit pale again. Has that DCI Hennessey upset you?" Elwyn asked as they made for the car.

"No, but I'm not sure what to make of her. She wanted to know about the bloke who spoke to me on Deansgate, the one who said those things about my parents. I want to be helpful, but it's a raw subject, Elwyn, and I've only just learned to live with it. For all I know he's just some villain I've had a run-in with that's stirring up trouble. Grim as it sounds, I'd rather that than Hennessey's scenario. She thinks there's some scam going on about what happened to my parents. He's done it to others too, apparently. She said this scam is linked to her current investigation but she wouldn't say more. I'm not sure what her angle is. I'll have to keep my eye on her."

"I'll do some checks, find out a bit more about her. You've enough to think about at the moment. I'd forget it, if I were you, otherwise it'll take over your head."

Good advice from Elwyn, as usual, but Rachel wasn't so sure. The DCI appeared to know her stuff. She wouldn't have come to see her without good reason. Rachel wanted to know what Nell Hennessey was investigating. Perhaps once this case was wrapped up, she'd speak to her again.

CHAPTER THIRTY-SIX

"I hope you appreciate our efforts," Jude said. "Jason and I have been burning the midnight oil all weekend on your behalf. Me here, stuck in the lab, and Jason at the mill."

Typical Jude. When she got involved, there was no stopping her. "You know we appreciate everything you do," Rachel said, smiling.

"Well, it's paid off. Examination of the bullets proves that Andy Siddall and Billy Sherwin were shot with the same gun."

Rachel had to admit that she hadn't even considered that one. She was slipping.

"But the big news is that over the weekend, Jason and his team found one of the bullets used to shoot Gavin Wellburn in the legs three years ago. Guess what we discovered?" Jude smiled. "It was a match to the other two."

Rachel took a few seconds to weigh this up. "You're saying that the same gun was used in all three shootings?"

"Exactly."

"Wellburn, Sherwin and Siddall, all with the same enemy. But who, and why?"

"Drugs?" suggested Elwyn. "We know Sherwin was heavily involved, perhaps the other two were running the show before him. This could be a simple matter of an argument between dealers."

"Where Sherwin's concerned, I agree, drugs could be the motive for his death, but we've found nothing to link either Wellburn or Siddall to his dealings. What does link them all, though, is Shawcross Mill," Rachel said thoughtfully.

"But why? What went on there that meant two men had to die and another be hospitalised?" Elwyn asked.

"I think Siddall was meant to die too, Elwyn. Have a word with those uniforms guarding him, make sure they stay sharp." She paused. "Anything on that Saint Christopher necklace found with the first body?"

"We have managed to extract DNA from the links in the chain, and it isn't the victim's. I think he must have wrenched it from around someone's neck and hung on to it," Jude said.

"Do we have a match?" Rachel asked.

Jude gave them her best disappointed look. "No."

Nonetheless, Jude and her team had done well. Rachel knew now that they were most likely looking for someone who was involved with Wellburn, Siddall and Sherwin. Given that everyone knew everyone else in the area around the mill, that wasn't surprising.

"What now?" Elwyn asked as they left.

"I'll get on to Amy about the jeweller's mark on that necklace. She was supposed to be chasing it up. They might have a record of who bought it. And I think we should have another word with Dylan Healey. He knew Sherwin and was terrified of the man. Now Sherwin's dead, he might be prepared to tell us more."

"We're going with the drugs angle then?" he asked.

Rachel climbed into the passenger seat. "We've got nothing else. Sherwin was a dealer. They were all shot with the same gun. This case has to involve drugs somewhere down the line. We'll go and see what Jason's found next."

Elwyn changed the subject. "Good weekend?"

"I had a visit from Jed on Sunday, that's partly why I didn't come in. We had a long talk about stuff."

He glanced at her. "Any *stuff* in particular?"

Rachel smiled. "I told him about the baby."

Elwyn gave a long whistle. "And he took it well?"

"I think so. He was surprised. But he's promised to do his share of the childcare. I doubt he'll be as good as Alan, but he reckons he's happy to put his all into it."

"Well, you really like to upend your whole life from one day to the next! Jed is constantly jetting about, eyeing up property. How will he cope with an infant and having to see a client at a moment's notice?" Elwyn asked.

"I don't know, but he's promised to make it work, and I'll keep him to that. But I do intend to take extended leave, so we'll have plenty of time to learn how to live together and develop a routine for the baby."

Elwyn's face fell. "I'm sorry to hear that," he said. "I realise you'll have to take time off, but I'm a selfish so-and-so. I was hoping it would be the minimum."

"It's the baby or my career, Elwyn. I've reached an age where I can't do both well. The pressures are too great. I did it once, but I was considerably younger, I had Alan on tap and the energy."

She could see that he was upset. They'd worked together for a long time and had an excellent clear-up rate. This could put paid to that.

"We'll get someone else for the duration," he said. "Any ideas? Please don't saddle me with a workshy useless idiot!"

"I might not have a say in the matter and I haven't discussed it with Kenton yet. I'm avoiding him because of the case. He'll have loads of tricky questions and I've got little in the way of answers. Tell him I'm pregnant and he'll use it as an excuse to hand the whole lot over to the cold case team. We've put in too much work to allow that to happen now."

"It won't be the same, coming in each day and you not being here."

"You'll have the team around you, and the work. The time will fly, Elwyn, you'll see. Meanwhile, I'll be up to my neck in nappies and baby sick. Don't expect me to feel sorry for you. I'll be back — I just don't know when."

CHAPTER THIRTY-SEVEN

Jonny Farrell looked through the statements that had been taken the previous week. Ray Pearce, Andy Siddall and Gavin Wellburn didn't have records. During interview, Siddall had mentioned having an altercation one night after drinking in a pub. They'd all drunk too much and had attacked a man on the street. The man had been injured and was taken to hospital. He'd given a comprehensive description of his attackers, including Gavin Wellburn's leather jacket. Within a day or two, Wellburn was brought in and named the others. But the victim, despite having been hospitalised, had not pressed charges. Jonny was wondering why. The injuries he'd sustained were nasty, including a broken arm necessitating several weeks off work. Not surprising, given that one of the perpetrators was Ray Pearce.

Jonny decided to find out more about the assault. He knew where the victim worked from the record made at the time and decided to go and speak to him. He was curious as to why he'd taken no action, and wondered if that crew had leaned on him.

Amy was engrossed in something at her desk. "What are you up to?" Jonny asked.

"I'm trying to find out who that Saint Christopher was made for. The boss is on my back. I'm hoping the mark on it will give us something," Amy said.

"Any luck?"

"Nothing."

"Could it have been made by one of those craftspeople in the units at the mill?" he asked.

"It's worth a look." She smiled. "Thanks, Jonny."

"If the boss comes back, tell her I'll be about an hour," he said.

"You've found something," she said. "I know that look. Want to share?"

"Not yet, it might be nothing. But if it is, it might give us the break we need."

Amy frowned — he was at it again. "Stay in touch. The boss won't like it if you get into bother again."

Laughing, Jonny left the office. Eric Tunstall, the man who'd been assaulted, worked in a hardware shop on Levenshulme's high street. Not far, so with luck he should be there and back well within the hour.

He'd rung ahead and knew that Tunstall was working today, although he'd not said why he wanted to speak to him. Jonny didn't know if a chat would be useful or not, but when he'd read the report, his instinct had kicked in. The incident was important for some reason, and he wanted to find out more about it.

* * *

Tunstall was nervous. Jonny saw it the minute he introduced himself.

"Serious case, is it? Only I get a bit twitchy answering questions," Tunstall said.

"No need. Think of this as more a friendly chat," Jonny said. "You might be able to help me with something. Will you tell me about the night you were attacked by those blokes in town? The time you ended up in hospital with the broken arm?"

Tunstall's eyes narrowed. "Why d'you need to know about that? It was a while ago, over three years. What bearing can it have on anything now?"

"Please, Mr Tunstall, indulge me. Tell me what happened."

"Well, it was unprovoked. We all left the pub at closing time. I was on my way back towards my house and they set about me for no reason. There were three of them, I stood no chance. I ended up on the pavement semi-conscious. Spent two days laid up in hospital and I couldn't work for a while. It put me right off going out for ages."

"It was a nasty attack. The police arrested the men who'd assaulted you, but you wouldn't press charges, and that's what puzzled me. Will you tell me why?"

Tunstall shook his head. "Leave me alone. I don't like being interrogated like this. If you don't mind, I don't want to answer any more of your questions."

"It's hardly an interrogation, Mr Tunstall," Jonny protested. "I'm just after a few answers." He paused, giving the man time to think. "You must have lost money, having to take time off work. Did they threaten you, say they'd hurt you again if you didn't do as you were told?"

"No, I never saw them again after the attack. I described them to the police, and they were picked up. I identified them from photographs."

"You're quite sure it was them?" Jonny asked.

"Yes, I know who attacked me. I don't understand. Why ask me about all that now?"

"I'm curious as to why you let them get away with it, that's all."

"Have they attacked someone else?"

"They are involved in our current enquiries. Anything you tell me could help us."

Tunstall looked troubled. "My wife always said it would come back to haunt me. She was dead set against it from the start."

"Dead set against what, Mr Tunstall?"

He was silent for a while. "I was warned off, told not to say anything, and I was paid to keep quiet. They said I must act confused and drop all charges."

"You were paid? How much?"

"Five thousand pounds. For a man in my position, it was too good to refuse."

Jonny was surprised. He'd not reckoned with that one. "Who paid you? One of your attackers?"

"I don't know, but I reckon it must have been. I got a letter stuck through my door with instructions to drop all charges and I'd get paid. They kept their word, too. Within hours of sorting things with the police, the five grand was shoved through my letterbox."

"Do you still have the instructions or the packaging the cash was wrapped in?" asked Jonny.

"Of course I haven't. It was three years ago," Tunstall said. "I pocketed the cash and the wrapping went straight in the bin."

"Shame. They might have helped identify who paid you and where the money came from."

"They must have withdrawn it from the bank. The notes were new. I did jot down some of the serial numbers," he said, surprising Jonny. "I'm a bit of nerd that way, car number plates, that sort of thing. The notes were fifties, all sequential. I think I still have them at home in a notebook. Do you want me to drop it off at the station later?"

Jonny could barely believe his luck. "Yes, please — the station in Ancoats. Mark it for the attention of DC Farrell."

CHAPTER THIRTY-EIGHT

Dr Jason Fox and his team had done a great job with the tunnel. "We've lit the entire length of it," he told Rachel and Elwyn, "and removed all the debris that was blocking it, so it's a lot easier to navigate now."

"Where does it lead?" asked Elwyn

"Number forty-five, Redhill Terrace, Ancoats — well, to a flagstone in the cellar to be precise," Jason said.

The address wasn't known to them. "When we get back, see if there's a connection to anyone involved in this case," Rachel told Elwyn. "Is that where the old brickyard was years ago?"

"Not quite. The brickyard was further on," Jason said. "Someone deliberately chose to put an exit point there — an empty house, a back yard with high walls and a good size cellar. The way into the tunnel was lined with concrete and covered with a stone slab. Easy to miss unless you knew about it."

"And this was done within the last three years?" Elwyn asked.

"It's difficult to say, but I would think so."

Rachel was trying to weigh up the significance of what Jason had told them. There had to be a good reason to build the exit in that house in particular.

"Are there people living in the house?" she asked.

"No, thankfully. It would have hindered our investigation, and can you imagine the surprise when one of my forensic team popped up in the middle of the cellar?"

Rachel didn't know what to make of it. "Did you find anything else down there?"

"We've bagged everything we picked up and we'll go through it at the lab. Interestingly, among the litter were several chocolate bar and sandwich wrappers, along with an assortment of soft drink cans. The sandwiches had rotted away but the expiry dates on the wrappers were still visible. Guess when they were?" Jason smiled.

"The week in question? The time Wellburn was killed?"

"Yes. Someone was down here, for whatever reason, just at the time your victim was murdered. There is no doubt about it."

That meant the tunnel was significant. "This has to be Sherwin's work," Rachel said. "He must have used the tunnel to get his drugs in and out of the mill without being seen."

"Not recently, he didn't," Elwyn said. "The mill end was bricked up, with Wellburn's body behind it. And we still haven't determined how long Sherwin's been dealing."

But Rachel was insistent. "Sherwin must have used the tunnel. It's the only scenario that makes any sense. Things got tricky at the mill end, Wellburn was killed and Sherwin had to stop, find another way."

"And Wellburn?" Elwyn said. "He was shot with the same gun as Sherwin. No, Rachel, I think we're looking for someone else, another member of this gang we haven't reckoned with yet. Perhaps the one in that balaclava."

"We'll find out who's lived in the house over the past few years, see if that gives us something to go on," she said.

"Is it far?" Elwyn asked.

"No, a five-minute walk tops," Jason told him.

Elwyn looked at Rachel. "Shall we?"

"You shouldn't have any trouble," Jason said. "The tunnel's been swept, and the lights are on. You can't get lost. Some of my people are at the other end, they'll help you out."

"Weird, don't you think?" Rachel said. "Sherwin, or one of the gang, must have used this tunnel to avoid being seen. But I still don't understand. They've not been shy about using the main gates recently, so what's changed?"

* * *

A short walk later, they climbed the ladder into the house. Rachel looked around at the empty cellar and then went outside into the yard. The house was in a terrace and the yard was small. There wasn't much to see. "The surrounding walls are higher than usual and there's no gate," she noted.

"There's houses on the other side of that wall." Elwyn pointed. "That's why."

"Where're the dustbins?" Rachel asked.

Elwyn shrugged. "They're usually kept at the front, by the door."

Rachel walked through the house and out the front door. "So, an old cobbled backstreet in Ancoats. It goes nowhere."

Elwyn nodded at the bollards at one end that blocked off access to the main road. "There are no houses on the other side of the road, just a brick wall to keep people off the spare land behind it."

"No way out other than the front door," Rachel noted. "This street is short — what are there, a dozen houses? It's the sort of place where everyone knows what goes on. A word with the neighbours might be useful. People round here have long memories."

"They're all out, or not answering the door," Jason told her. "Except for an elderly man at the end and he's hard of hearing."

Nevertheless, Rachel intended to get Amy, Jonny and a couple of uniforms on it later. "We'll have a word with

Mathew Shawcross, see if he knows anything about the lay-out of the tunnel."

"We did find something else," Jason told them. "I'll show you on the way back. There's graffiti on the tunnel wall about halfway down — the names 'Rita' and 'Gav' inscribed in a heart and written in chalk."

That could only be Rita Pearce and their victim, Gavin Wellburn. Wellburn must be the other man Siddall had alluded to.

"Dylan Healey might be more willing to talk now that Sherwin's dead. He's been kicking around the mill for years. He might know something," Elwyn said.

"We'll bring him in," Rachel said.

* * *

Back at the station, Jonny was waiting for Rachel. "I've got something, ma'am. Do you recall that Siddall told us about a fight that ended with Gavin Wellburn and his chums being brought in?"

Rachel had forgotten about that. The incident was now just a small note, buried amidst all the others on the board.

"I don't know why but it bothered me, so I went and spoke to the victim, one Eric Tunstall. It turns out he was paid not to press charges," Jonny told her.

That made it far more interesting. "Siddall said nothing about that. Does Tunstall know who paid him the money?" Rachel asked.

"Afraid not, but the notes were fifties and new. The serial numbers were sequential. He noted them and brought them in for me on his way back to work after his lunch break."

Jonny reached for a notebook on his desk. "It's not all of them. At the time he'd no idea it would prove to be impor-tant, but look." He pointed. "The gap there, there's five notes missing. I've checked them against the serial numbers on the notes found in Wellburn's teeth, and I think they're a match."

"We don't have the complete numbers of the notes Jude found, just the odd few from scraps," Rachel reminded him.

"It's too much of a coincidence. Look, here." He showed her. "The partials we've deciphered and those Eric Tunstall, the bloke injured that night, gave us."

Jonny was right. That meant that whoever had paid off Tunstall must have had a hand in the murder of Wellburn. "We need another chat with Andy Siddall. He was there that night. He can tell us what this is all about."

"Five thousand," Elwyn said. "It's a lot of money. Where did it come from?"

"I've been on to the bank, and they should have an answer for us later. With the notes being new and sequential, they reckon they can trace who drew that money out," Jonny said.

CHAPTER THIRTY-NINE

Rachel's mobile rang. It was Jed. "I'll take this in my office." She went in and closed the door. "Is it important? I'm working."

"I thought you should know, your plan is working, Alan's moving out. He's got a removal firm in this morning and they're packing up his stuff. Apparently, it's going into storage until he and his lady move into the new house."

Alan had said nothing to Rachel, which was odd. All she could think of was that it was down to him having a guilty conscience about the whole thing. Ordinarily he would never sell to anyone, and particularly not Jed, but being with Belinda had changed him. The woman must have some influence, Rachel decided.

He was down to see to the girls today, including getting tea. "He'll be moving in with Belinda, then. I'll give him a ring. I hope he's not forgotten that it's his turn to feed the girls tonight. Since he decided to get hitched, he's not been the same, suddenly he's forgotten his responsibilities."

"I can give them dinner, if you don't object."

"They need feeding properly, Jed, not on takeaways, and there's Mia's stuff to sort for tomorrow. She's got netball and needs her kit. Knowing that girl, I bet it's still in the washing basket."

"None of that is beyond me, Rachel. I do look after myself pretty well, you know. And I've been thinking. How would you feel if I moved in with you until the legal stuff with Alan is sorted? I'd be on hand to cope with the girls, leaving you free to work. I did spend that time with them on Anglesey, it's not as if we're strangers."

Rachel's first thought was to refuse outright. Jed and her, under the same roof? She couldn't see it working. On the other hand, having him seeing to meals and the girls instead of Alan would take a weight off her shoulders. Megan was due to move out anytime and that would leave Mia alone. Alan was bound to be busy during the coming weeks. Rachel was tempted, but then she brought herself up short — this was Jed talking about moving in. "You'd hate it. They're a demanding pair. Give them an inch and they'll be running rings around you."

"I realise I've got no experience of parenting, Rachel, but how hard can it be? What d'you say?"

Did she have much choice? Jed was determined and Alan was under some spell Belinda had woven around him. There was no let up in the current case and Rachel could do without the added problem of the kids. She smiled. He'd no idea! But when she boiled it down, what harm could it do? It would be good practice for when the baby came. "Okay, you can have the spare room at the back of the house. You're making the tea tonight, from scratch. And make sure Mia has a clean school shirt and PE kit for tomorrow."

"I won't let you down," he said. "When will you be home?"

"I've no idea. Put something by and I'll eat later."

There was a knock on her office door. Elwyn wanted her. "Got to go," she said to Jed. "Don't destroy my kitchen and keep the food simple."

Rachel beckoned to Elwyn. "Sorry, a little domestic stuff to sort."

"We've got a problem. Siddall has discharged himself. He's not at home and no one's seen him."

159

Rachel groaned — this was all they needed. "What about the uniforms watching him?"

"Apparently Siddall put on a set of scrubs and got out while they were talking to a nurse."

"Bloody useless. The man's in danger."

"He's likely to go to Rita Pearce. The pair are close, and she could well be sheltering him."

"Mathew Shawcross, Dylan Healey and now Rita Pearce. We need to speak to them all, Elwyn. We're going to be here until the death tonight."

CHAPTER FORTY

Rita Pearce stood behind the bar at the Spinners Arms, sick with fear. Her husband, Ray, had just thrown Dylan Healey, known locally as 'Spider,' out on to the street. The lad had gone headfirst on to the pavement, scraping his face on the tarmac and rolling into the gutter.

"Bloody liability, that kid. Don't let him back in," Ray roared at his wife. "You saw what he was doing?"

Trembling, Rita shook her head. She was waiting for the pain of his fist, or for him to grab her arm and shake her until she fell. But he'd been drinking and wasn't so steady on his feet.

"Smoking bloody weed in my pub, that's what! Silly bitch! You turn a blind eye far too often. We get caught with the likes of him doing as they please in here and we're finished."

"Sorry, Ray." Her voice shook. "I was busy."

"Busy doing bugger all. I should knock your bloody head off."

"You lay a finger on her, Ray Pearce, and I'll sort you once and for all."

The voice came from the doorway. Rita looked up, startled. It was Andy Siddall. He shouldn't be here — he wasn't well enough. "No, Andy, please. Don't take him on."

Normally, Siddall could handle himself but in his weakened state, Ray might do him irreparable damage. "What are you doing out of hospital?" she asked.

"I'm okay. Don't you worry about me." He looked at Ray. "Back off, or I'll flatten you."

"Brave words. I'd like to see you try," Ray sneered. "You won't touch me, you're too bloody yellow. I know you of old, remember?"

Siddall moved closer, thrust his face forward. "You're not so tough yourself these days, Ray. You drink too much and you're flabby. Want to risk it?"

Rita saw her husband back off a couple of paces, saw the rage in his dark eyes. Ray wouldn't take insults like this lying down.

"Get out of my pub. Come in here again and I'll kill you."

"Rita," Siddall called to her. "You don't have to stay here with him. Get your stuff and we'll leave together."

Ray Pearce slammed his fist on the bar. "She's going nowhere with you, or anyone else."

Rita watched, hardly daring to breath, as Andy Siddall advanced to within an inch of Ray's face. "That's up to her. Now back off or you'll come off worst."

Rita couldn't take any more. Ray was likely to snap at any second. If he did, he wouldn't hold back. Just as Ray Pearce raised his fist to punch Siddall, Rita darted between the two men. Ray lashed out, his fist connected with her stomach and she fell to the floor.

"Happy now?" Ray sneered. He raised a booted foot and kicked her. "Get up, woman. C'mon. Work to do."

His voice reached Rita from a distance. She gasped for breath. The pain in her side was excruciating. She tried to raise herself up but sank to the floor again. Her head was swimming, she couldn't think. The last thing she saw was Andy's concerned face, and then she lost consciousness.

"Get an ambulance!" Siddall screamed. "You've bloody knocked her out."

* * *

Rachel and Elwyn arrived at the pub to see Ray Pearce rooted to the spot, staring down at his wife who was lying on the floor. The place was empty. Anyone who'd been drinking there had left. Andy Siddall was bent over Rita, trying to wake her. She lay, still and silent, and didn't respond.

"I've been trying to rouse her for ages but she hasn't moved," he sobbed.

Rachel sprang forward and got down on her knees to check on her. "What happened?"

"Him and his fists." Siddall nodded at Pearce. "He thumped her."

"Has anyone rung an ambulance?" Elwyn asked.

"I did," Siddall said. "That stupid sod has lost his tongue."

Ray Pearce tore his eyes away from Rita. "She got in the way," he mumbled. "That punch was meant for him, not her."

"Elwyn," Rachel whispered. "There are uniforms across the road guarding the mill, get a couple over here. Ray Pearce is coming with us."

Rita didn't look good. She appeared to have trouble breathing and her lips were blue. "He hit her hard?" she asked Siddall.

"Yes, caught her right here." He pointed to the spot on his own body. "He's a heavy man. Those fists — God knows what damage he's done."

Rachel was concerned that Rita might have a ruptured spleen, or some other internal damage. She was thin, and had no meat on her bones to protect her.

Pearce was standing by the bar, looking dazed. "I didn't mean it, she knows that. Rita and me, we have an understanding."

Siddall looked him in the eye. "And we know exactly what that is, don't we, mate? Don't like her behaviour or her attitude and you curb it with violence. You've never been any different."

Rachel looked up at Elwyn. "See how far away that ambulance is, she's not good." Rachel took hold of Rita's hand. Poor woman, she had a hard life. Rachel couldn't understand why she stayed. The pub was in dire need of renovation. With its walls of dingy brown paint, it had a depressing ugliness about it. Rachel doubted the living quarters were much different.

"Don't worry, Rita," she whispered. "Help's on its way." To her huge relief, minutes later the ambulance arrived.

CHAPTER FORTY-ONE

Eyes on the floor, Ray Pearce sat with his solicitor opposite Rachel and Elwyn. He was subdued, the blustering bully from the Spinners Arms had disappeared.

"What is it between you and Andy Siddall?" Elwyn began.

"Rita," he said simply. "Him and her, they're close, and I won't stand for it. It was bad enough when she had a thing for Wellburn, now Siddall seems to have taken his place."

"That's no reason to try to thump him," Rachel said.

"You have no idea. Siddall is a piece of work. You don't know him like I do."

"Well, you made a big mistake this time, Ray," Elwyn said. "You will be charged with assault on your wife."

He shrugged, cocky again. "She won't press charges. Once Rita's fixed up, she'll come home, like she always does."

"You're very sure of that," Rachel said.

"She won't go with Siddall if that's what you're thinking. Yeah, they're close, but Rita won't leave me. Rita's problem is she's not independent enough, can't manage on her own. If she could, she'd have walked out years ago."

"So, you're certain about the charges," Elwyn said.

Ray Pearce looked at him as if he was stupid.

"I'll talk her round. Bunch of flowers, you know. Rita's easily swayed." He grinned.

"Sooner or later, Ray, Rita will get sick and tired of being your punchbag," Rachel said.

"Not this time. She'll come home, you'll see."

Ray Pearce seemed to be under the illusion that if Rita didn't press charges, they had little or no chance of keeping him. That wasn't true, but it would save time if Rita cooperated. And right now, more than anything, Rachel wanted this man locked up. Clipping Ray Pearce's wings was the only way to keep Rita safe from harm.

There was a knock on the door. Amy, wanting an urgent word with Rachel. She was holding several sheets of paper and looked excited.

"I've found something, ma'am, it's important," Amy said.

Rachel joined her in the corridor. "Can't it wait until we've finished with Pearce?"

"No, ma'am, you need to hear this."

Amy took a sheet from the papers and thrust it towards Rachel. "That house on Redhill Terrace, the one at the end of the tunnel?"

Rachel nodded. "Go on."

"About three years ago, Ray Pearce rented the place for a few weeks. And it fits our timescale for the murder." Amy smiled triumphantly.

Rachel gave her a pat on the back. This was exactly what was needed. "Good work, Amy, you've done well." Rachel looked at the sheet. "Do we know who owns the house?"

"The Shawcross Estate."

That was interesting, but it didn't surprise Rachel. Redhill Terrace wasn't that far from the mill and at one time the estate had owned all the houses in the area. This new information meant that even if Rita didn't press charges, they had enough on Ray Pearce to hang on to him while further investigations were carried out. What they wanted now was to know why he'd rented the house and if it had anything to do with Wellburn's murder.

Rachel returned to the interview room and sat down. After a few moments' silence, she handed the sheet to Elwyn and gave him a wink.

"Okay, Mr Pearce. Redhill Terrace. Why did you need to rent a house when you already had a home?"

Pearce's eyes widened and he turned pale. "I didn't. You've made a mistake."

"No. We have the documentation here." She put down the paper in front of him. "You rented the house for a period of one month. It says so here."

He shrugged. "So? I'd forgotten. It was a while ago. Me and Rita weren't getting on. I rented it as a bolthole in case we split up. The tenancy of the Spinners Arms is in her name, so if things got tricky it'd be me that would have to leave."

Sounded plausible enough, but he was lying. His body language spoke volumes. He shifted in his seat, played with his hands and he couldn't look her in the face.

"There's a flagstone in the cellar of that house," Rachel said. "It leads down into a tunnel that goes directly to Shawcross Mill."

Pearce glanced at his solicitor. "Where's this rubbish coming from? A tunnel, you say. That's all very interesting, but it has nothing to do with me. I never actually moved into that address, ask anyone. Me and Rita sorted things out and I was able to get out of the lease."

"I don't believe you, Mr Pearce," Rachel said. "We found a body in that tunnel, that of a man known to have been in a relationship with your wife. That gives you a motive. You'll be staying here until we've completed our enquiries."

"I want to make that phone call now."

"Certainly. The desk sergeant will arrange it. Who do you want to speak to?" Rachel asked.

"Mathew Shawcross," Pearce said.

CHAPTER FORTY-TWO

Ray Pearce's request threw Rachel completely. Why him? Unless he wanted to speak to Mathew Shawcross because he would have been the landlord at the time Pearce had rented the house, but even so. "What possible relationship can that pair have?" she asked the team. "And more to the point, why does Pearce think that Shawcross will help him?" She looked round at their blank faces. "C'mon. Doesn't anyone have a theory?"

"I think someone is orchestrating the drug dealing," Elwyn said. "Sherwin was the public face, but Pearce could have been the one running things. He was close enough to the mill, the pub is right across the street. We know that Millie Shawcross and her boyfriend were involved with Sherwin — essentially, he was blackmailing them to do his bidding. If I'm right then Pearce will know this and thinks he can now manipulate Shawcross, persuade the man to help him."

"You mean to keep his daughter out of it? You think perhaps Millie was more involved than we were led to believe?" said Rachel.

"With regard to the dealing, who knows? But it wouldn't surprise me. Her boyfriend is an addict," Jonny said.

"And as you pointed out in there, Pearce does have a motive for killing Gavin Wellburn," Elwyn said. "He's a jealous man, controlling. If he found out about Rita's affair, he's the type who would lash out."

"Lashing out is one thing, but Wellburn was shot in both legs and left to rot. It was hardly a spur-of-the-moment killing," Rachel said.

"I still don't understand why Pearce needed the house on Redhill Terrace, or the tunnel," Jonny said. "Until we put a stop to it, drugs were going in and out of that mill all the time — through the front gates."

Jonny had a point. She'd been struggling with that one too. That house had been rented because a hole could be dug from the cellar intersecting with the tunnel leading to the mill. That was a lot of work, and right now, Rachel could see no reason for it. But someone must have thought it worthwhile enough to put in the hard labour.

"Did you find anything on that address?" she asked Elwyn.

"Sorry, Rachel, I've not had the time," Elwyn said.

"Stella," Rachel called out. "Do a comprehensive search for anything we've got on that address in Redhill Terrace. Jonny, Amy, go and find Dylan Healey and bring him in. We'll see if he is feeling more talkative now that Sherwin's dead. He knows that area and everything that goes on there. Elwyn and I will go and speak to Shawcross."

Rachel glanced at the office clock. It was gone four in the afternoon — the traffic would be heavy. "Sorry, this will take a while. Have you got plans?"

Elwyn pulled a face and shook his head. "No, you?"

"I'd better ring home, check in."

"Do we call and tell Shawcross we're coming?"

"No. Let's surprise him."

* * *

"Everything okay at home?" Elwyn asked as they negotiated the traffic queuing to get on to the Kingsway roundabout.

"Couldn't be better. Seems Jed has a domestic side I was totally unaware of. Hope he keeps it up. He's staying with us while the legal stuff for next door is completed," Rachel said.

"You've moved him in? That didn't take long."

"He's in the spare room and that's where he's staying," Rachel said firmly. "Although I will admit, he's surprised me. He seems happy enough to slot into my mad family and help where he can. The baby hasn't fazed him either."

Elwyn smiled. "That's good news but what about the girls, how are they taking it?"

"Mia is delighted, she took to Jed from the off. Megan, I'm not so sure how that will pan out. For the time being she's hardly home, too busy shifting her stuff into her mate's flat in town. I did try to have the conversation but her head's full of other stuff."

"All you have to do now is tell Kenton and arrange your maternity leave. How long will you take? I have to admit, your use of the word 'extended' had me bothered."

"I'm still weighing that one up, but you deserve the truth, Elwyn. If Jed and I do make a go of it, and it works, I won't be rushing back. I'll go off as soon as I can and once the baby comes, I intend to take at least a year."

Elwyn's face fell. "Makes sense. Jed McAteer can well afford to keep you."

"If I let him," Rachel said sharply. "I'm not marrying the man — well, not yet."

"Be sure you know what you're doing, Rachel. I don't want to see you get hurt."

Neither did she. And it was a gamble. Her relationship with Jed had always been volatile. Arguing was all very well when they were alone, but it wouldn't do to carry on like that in front of her daughters. Rachel turned to look at the passing countryside. A few miles out of the city and the scenery was completely different. The tall concrete buildings and traffic gave way to neat houses with gardens and trees. Even the sky looked bluer.

"Things will be different this time, Elwyn. I can feel it. Both me and Jed have learned a lot in the past years, particularly about what's really important."

They were turning into the drive of Shawcross's house. "How do we play this?" asked Elwyn.

"Carefully. We don't want to antagonise the man. I'm hoping he'll help us, talk to us candidly about Millie and what she's been up to."

"And if he doesn't?"

"We'll have to speak to the girl herself, and her boyfriend."

CHAPTER FORTY-THREE

Mathew Shawcross swore, then stared at the two detectives in angry silence. Rachel flinched. Maybe he genuinely didn't know what Millie had been up to. If he had, he was doing a damn good job of fooling them.

"You believe my daughter is involved with a known drug dealer? That she is in a relationship with an addict and buys drugs for him?" His voice rose.

"We realise it's a lot to take in, Mr Shawcross, but we know it to be true," Rachel said.

His face was red with rage. "There's no way she'd do that. Who is spreading these lies? Come on, who told you this rubbish about Millie, and who is this supposed dealer?"

"His name is Billy Sherwin. He was recently the victim of a fatal shooting. He did most of his dealing out of your mill in Ancoats. It is a regular haunt for addicts, and one of those is your daughter's boyfriend, Damon Brooke."

At the mention of the name, Shawcross turned even redder. "I warned her! I told Millie he was no good, but she's exactly like her mother, takes no notice and goes her own way."

"Have you heard the name Billy Sherwin before?" Elwyn asked him. "Has he ever contacted you, for example, asking for money?"

Shawcross's head shot up. "No! Why would he? Besides, he'd get nothing from me."

"Sherwin threatened people. He was a thug who thought nothing of using physical violence to intimidate his customers," Rachel said.

"Did he hurt Millie?" There was genuine fear in his eyes.

"No, we don't believe so, but he did force her to provide false alibis for him."

"Let me make something clear. I have never heard the name, and if Millie had come to me, we'd have told you lot straight away. That sort of business needs stamping out."

He looked rattled, but Rachel pushed on. She needed to get to the truth. "I am aware that you and Millie have had your problems in the past."

"That young detective's been gossiping, has he? He's no doubt given you the juicy lowdown on our private lives. Did he tell you she didn't even use the Shawcross name for years, choosing instead to use her mother's? Millie is hot-headed, acts before she thinks and has no sense of what's good for her. I had hoped she'd settled down. Fat chance of that. My heart sank when I learned she was seeing Brooke. I could tell from just looking at him that he was no good."

"You really didn't know about the drugs?" Elwyn asked.

"I said not, didn't I?" he retorted. "Bloody cheek, using my mill to sell the filthy stuff."

"Did you know about the tunnel?" Rachel said, changing tack.

"Yes, of course. You found that body in there. That tunnel is very old. It connects to the site of the old brickyard if I remember correctly."

Rachel nodded. "When was it last used?"

Shawcross gave a hollow laugh. "When the body was dumped in it, I imagine. Why do you ask?"

"Just curious." She smiled. "Have you ever been down there?"

"I've not been near that mill in years. Why would I? I'm not likely to now, either. It's on the market and I've finally got a developer interested in the land."

That was one to ask Jed about when she finally got home.

"Thank you for your time. We may need to speak to you again," Rachel said, getting to her feet. "One last thing. Do you know a man called Ray Pearce?"

"No, why? Who is he?"

"Currently he's under arrest and as such he is permitted to have someone notified of his arrest. He gave us your name as the person he wants to speak to. Do you know why he'd do that?" she asked.

"No idea. It has to be some sort of joke."

"I doubt that," Rachel said. "What he was arrested for is no joking matter."

Shawcross frowned. "Is Millie in any sort of trouble?"

"She lied for Sherwin, but since he did threaten her, I doubt much will come of it."

"I'll have the family lawyer on standby just in case. Millie is a lot of things, but she's my only child," Shawcross said. "Despite what she might have done, it's up to me to protect her."

* * *

"Well, that was a waste of time," Elwyn said, back at the incident room. "He told us nothing, didn't even admit to knowing Pearce."

"I can forgive that. He was angry about his daughter, but he certainly didn't tell us everything. I don't think Mathew Shawcross is as open and honest as I first thought. But if I'm right, what's he hiding?"

The incident room was empty except for Jonny. He was at his computer, ploughing through mobile phone records.

"Jonny, you've done your fair share today. Get off home," Rachel told him.

"I've got something, ma'am. These are Siddall's phone records. Everything is fairly standard, except for several calls to another mobile. No name, just a number, and it's not registered to anyone."

"You've tried calling it?"

"Yes, but it's turned off."

"We'll just have to ask Siddall himself then." Rachel thought for a moment. "Give that number to the tech people, see if they can help. They may be able to get a fix on where it's being used from, which mast it pinged, that type of thing." She looked at the clock. "But in the morning. It's getting late. Did we find Healey?"

"Not a trace of him, ma'am. He must have gone to ground since his fracas with Pearce."

"No matter, we'll deal with that tomorrow too." She turned to Elwyn. "I'm off home. Don't stay here until the death, either of you."

Rachel was looking forward to putting the case behind her for the evening. Jed would have a meal ready, and then the pair of them could discuss the future. That thought made her nervous. Rachel had often dreamed of a future with Jed but now that it was about to happen, she could see the problems. They needed to plan the way forward, thrash out some ground rules, stick to them and, hopefully, all would be well.

It was dark in the street. The light outside the station was out again. She walked the few metres to her car, dumped her stuff in the boot and was about to open the driver's door when she heard a voice behind her, making her jump.

"Like I told you the other night — your parents' crash was no accident. You're a detective, so investigate. He needs stopping."

He was right at her back, speaking into her ear. A splinter of fear ran down Rachel's spine. She turned to tackle him, but the man was gone as fast as he'd appeared. All she saw was those striped trainers flashing down the street.

CHAPTER FORTY-FOUR

Tuesday

Rachel woke to the aroma of bacon drifting upstairs. She lifted her head off the pillow and groaned. Normally, that smell'd make her mouth water. In fact it did today, but from nausea rather than pleasure.

Downstairs, Jed was hard at it, making breakfast for Mia. Very new and not altogether welcome. The kitchen looked as if he'd used every utensil she owned. What was wrong with shaking some cereal into a bowl?

"Want some?" he asked. "Start the day with a full belly, see you through to lunch without needing to snack."

"I don't snack," Rachel said.

"You used to. Back in the day, you were always munching on something — crisps or chocolate."

Mia smirked. "I'm surprised you're not humongous."

"Where's Megan?"

"At the flat. Said she'd be back at the weekend," Mia said.

"Get your stuff packed and then you can eat," Rachel told her.

"How's the case doing?" Jed asked. "Any chance of some time off?"

Rachel scraped back her hair and fastened it in a pony-tail. "I wish! We'll be lucky to sort this one in time for me giving birth."

"You should tell Kenton, warn him that you'll be taking time off."

"The case first, and then I'll deal with him," she said.

"Tea? Coffee? Something to eat?" Jed offered.

Rachel liked the way he'd made himself at home. He'd dived into her life feet first and wasn't doing badly at all. Mia was certainly happy. Jed would be a useful addition.

"Do you know Shawcross Mill?" she asked.

"That crumbling heap in Ancoats? Yes, why?"

"We found a body in there. The poor bloke had been dead a while."

"This the case you're working on?" he asked.

Rachel nodded, pouring herself some juice.

"How long'd he been dead?"

"About three years, Jude reckons," she said.

"Hidden, was it? The body?"

"Oh yes. Whoever left the poor bugger there definitely didn't want him found," she said.

Jed smiled. "Interesting case. Something to get your teeth into."

Rachel watched him for a few moments. "Do you know something? Because if you do, tell me."

"I know the owner isn't as squeaky clean as he makes out. His daughter mixes with some dubious types, a notorious drug dealer, for a start."

"I'd no idea you knew the Shawcross family," she said.

Jed shrugged. "I don't, but I've heard rumours."

That had Rachel interested. "Care to share them?"

"Not really. Probably a load of rubbish anyway."

"Go on," she said. "Indulge me while I get some cereal."

"He's the jealous type, is Shawcross, and I don't just mean in a mild way either. Do him down, cross him in any way, and he doesn't forget or forgive. If he can get even, he will. Ask his ex-wife. She'll give you a better picture than I can."

Rachel made a mental note. A word with the woman might be worthwhile. "The mill is up for sale," Rachel said. "What d'you reckon?"

Jed pondered this for a minute. "Ancoats is a desirable location these days, particularly for apartments in revamped old cotton mills. I'd say it was a good investment for someone."

If that was the case, why hadn't Mathew Shawcross tried to cash in on the mill before now? All that tripe he'd spouted about the family history was just that. Tripe. There had to be something else. The body, perhaps?

"I'm going for a shower. Work could be heavy going today, so I can't say when I'll be back. Will you be able to cope?" she said.

Jed nodded. Rachel made her way back upstairs with a smile on her face. This was something of a baptism of fire for him — full on family life and not much respite. She almost felt sorry for him.

* * *

Rachel was about to drive away from the house when her mobile rang. It was Nell Hennessey, the DCI from Tameside. "You had another visit from our unknown friend last night," she said. "You should have rung me."

"Look, I don't know what this is about, but I don't have time to deal with it right now. I'm up to my eyeballs in a complex murder case. Perhaps in a few days." Rachel paused. "How did you know anyway?"

"He sent me a text to say he'd seen you. We need to speak, Rachel."

Hadn't the woman heard her? "It can't be today, I've got interviews and statements to plough through."

"Rachel, this is a serious matter. Meet me for lunch — your canteen."

She wasn't going to give up. "You'll have to take your chances," Rachel said. "But I'll do my best."

"I'll be there about one."

The woman was becoming a nuisance, but Rachel couldn't help being curious. The man who'd approached her — what did he want? And why tell her that tale about her parents? Maybe she'd have to make time for Nell Hennessey. Whatever she knew, Rachel was determined to get it out of her.

CHAPTER FORTY-FIVE

Rachel gathered the team together in the incident room for a briefing. They had a board full of information and a whole stack of statements, but they were still no nearer finding who had killed Gavin Wellburn and Billy Sherwin and injured Andy Siddall. Currently, their prime suspect was Ray Pearce, but they needed proof to back it up.

"I want Pearce's alibis checking for both Sherwin's murder and the attack on Siddall. Amy, I'll leave that to you. And don't accept any vague excuses about serving in the Spinners Arms. That pub isn't busy and it's almost always Rita who's behind the bar. I want a solid timeframe for that man's movements."

She looked at Jonny. "I want you to take a couple of uniforms and knock on every door in Redhill Terrace. Find out anything you can about that house, any incident on that street within the last three years. It's only a few metres long and blocked off at one end. I suspect that anything goes on along there and everyone knows about it. Stella, have you found anything?"

"There was an incident a while ago involving the police. DCI Lennox from Central attended. They found the body of a murder victim at that address."

A piece of information that could possibly open another can of worms. First thing was to ascertain if that murder was in any way related to their current investigation. "Timescale?" Rachel asked.

"Fits with our investigation. Just short of three years ago."

Coincidence? Rachel thought not. This meant even more work. That case would have to be looked at, statements gone through, the works. "Dig out the case file, would you, Stella? I'll have a look later. Jonny, while you're on that street, find out what you can about it. The immediate neighbours are bound to know something — if the victim was local, someone they knew, for example."

Next, she turned to Elwyn. "You and I will go over everything we've got so far. We still don't know what links these men together — apart from the mill, that is. And before you say anything, I don't think it's drugs."

Kenton came in and stood at the back of the room. He didn't look pleased. Well, she was in no mood to take flak from him.

"Progress?" he asked.

"We're getting there."

"You have a man in the cells. Is he your killer? Remember what I said about the time limit for this case? You are running close to the wire and costs are rising."

Had they been alone, he would have had the sharp end of her tongue, but not in front of the team. Why couldn't he wait another couple of days before throwing his weight around? They were still short of solid evidence. A little longer and they would have this wrapped up.

"We have two historic murders, one current, and a serious wounding, all carried out using the same gun. Our investigation, including gathering the evidence that will make the CPS happy, is complicated." Rachel took a breath. "Sir. I'll give you a further update later today."

Kenton could take it or leave it. Rachel couldn't work with him breathing down her neck.

"My office, when you've finished here," he said.

So that's how it was going to be. She sighed. "Okay, team, get to it."

"Tell him about the baby," Elwyn whispered as she passed. "It will defuse the situation if things get awkward."

"If he gets awkward I'm likely to slap him one! We're working flat out here, Elwyn, and he damn well knows it. That little show was pure old-style Kenton. That man likes to throw his weight around, show everyone who's boss. Well he won't get away with it, not with me."

"Take a breath and have a coffee or something. Don't go in there all guns blazing, that's not the way to deal with him."

Good advice, and well worth listening to, but not today. "I'm off coffee, as you know." With an apologetic smile to Elwyn, Rachel made for Kenton's office.

* * *

"For the sake of the station's budget, I need this case sorted urgently, Rachel," Kenton began without any preliminaries. "No doubt you feel aggrieved by my insistence, but you have no idea of the pressure I'm under from them upstairs."

Kenton was at his desk, a spreadsheet open on his computer screen. Rachel sat down opposite him. "Not my problem, Mark. I catch villains, killers, and they have a habit of upsetting police budgets."

"Okay, I take your point, but I repeat, the body found in that mill should have been handed over to the cold case team. If you'd taken my advice, we wouldn't be having this conversation now."

"We have one new killing and one serious wounding related to that original case, so I was right. Gavin Wellburn's murder is irrefutably relevant to the past week's shootings of both Billy Sherwin and Andy Siddall."

"Motive?"

"We've been looking at drug dealing, but now I'm not so sure. Sherwin was a dealer, a major player in the area, but

182

not the others. They weren't even users. However, the one thing that does link them all is that mill."

"I read in the reports about the tunnel. That is interesting. A lot of work was done to make it useable, that has to be important. I take it you are exploring why an exit was built in the cellar of that house and what its purpose was?"

Rachel nodded. "Of course, but so far we can find no reason for it. One of my team is questioning the residents of that street today. With luck he may turn up something. Part of the delay is down to having to wait while the tunnel was rendered safe. As it was, it was a health and safety nightmare."

Rachel waited for his reply. Surely he had to see sense given everything she'd told him. She just hoped he didn't ask how much longer, because until they had answers to key questions, she'd no idea.

He nodded. "Okay, given what you've got, carry on with the good work. I'll need another update later today."

Rachel nodded — she'd got what she wanted. Kenton had a job to do but he also understood what those on the ground were up against. When he'd been a detective at Salford, Kenton had had an excellent clear-up rate, so he must appreciate what that took. Maybe she could keep him onside after all.

CHAPTER FORTY-SIX

Taking two uniformed officers with him, Jonny went to Redhill Terrace. They visited every house, knocked on every door and spoke to all the residents. He decided to concentrate on the immediate neighbours himself, reckoning that they were the best bet.

Arthur and Elsie Michaels lived at number forty-seven. Arthur answered the door and Jonny introduced himself. "Would you mind answering some questions about the house next door?" he asked.

The elderly man's eyes lit up, and he immediately invited Jonny in. "Me and the wife are pleased to help if we can. Come on through. I always suspected that incident was a long way from being resolved. Mind you, these days it's as quiet as the grave round 'ere. I should know, been 'ere nigh on forty years. And there's not much goes on that gets past me and the wife, I can tell you. She's in t' kitchen, come and sit down and she'll make you a cuppa. We don't get many visitors. Kids are grown up and live away and grandkids don't bother much."

Jonny wondered if this was a good idea after all. Probably the man was just desperate to talk to someone, and interviewing him could be a huge waste of time. Still, he had to try, find out what he knew. He followed Arthur through to the sitting room.

The rooms were small and the furniture old-fashioned. Everything had seen better days, and some of the items were obviously several decades old. But the battered sofa was comfortable, and the open fire was warm and welcoming.

Arthur called through to the kitchen. "Elsie! Come and meet this young man. Always up to her elbows in the sink that one. It's washday today. She likes her routine, bless her."

The woman was tiny, with short curly hair and twinkly blue eyes. In her frilly apron, she reminded Jonny of the archetypal granny you see in kid's storybooks.

"This is a detective," her husband said. "He's asking about the house next door and the folk who lived there, that type of thing."

"You want to know about that poor bloke who was murdered, you mean? I thought that was all done with a while ago."

"Tell me about that, Mrs Michaels."

"We heard them arguing. Going at it for ages, they were. They were shouting and throwing things about, and then we heard the shot." She looked at her husband. "We didn't know what to do. Arthur wanted to go round but I stopped him and we rang the police instead."

"You did the right thing. You could have got hurt yourself."

"Next thing, we've got armed police hammering at the door. I wouldn't have minded but they were too late." She looked at her husband. "We heard that second shot and we just knew, didn't we, Arthur?"

Jonny had only glimpsed the details on the system. He wanted to know more. "Can you tell me exactly what happened?" he asked them. "Did you see the victim go into the house?"

"No, but the kids around here did. They were playing out in the street, and they remembered him because he gave them a mouthful about keeping away from his car."

"What about the killer?" asked Jonny.

"It's still unsolved," Arthur said. "The killer is the mystery. No one saw him go into that house or leave, for that matter. Take a look across the road." Arthur pointed to the top of the wall opposite. "There's a camera up there, focused on the street. The police got nothing from it. One of your lot said the killer must have got in through the back, but there was no evidence of that either. We had forensics people all over the back yards for days." Arthur laughed. "Have you seen the back of these houses? No way out at all. A high wall and then more houses. It is well nigh impossible to scale something that high. Anyway, even if the killer had tried, he'd have been seen by the neighbours. One thing we do have round here, lad, is twitchy curtains."

"Do you know who the victim was?" Jonny asked

"Gordon Swan, the bookie. He owned half a dozen betting shops around Manchester and four in Salford."

"And he was killed next door?" Jonny said incredulously. Why hadn't one of team heard of this? Back then this area came under a different station, his own team at East Manchester were no doubt up to their ears in something of their own.

He'd heard of Swan, knew his reputation. The man had been a hard-hearted, and extremely successful businessman who'd run a tight ship. Jonny could see no reason for him to be in this tiny corner of Ancoats, never mind get shot here.

"Had he ever lived around here? Did he know the place?" Jonny asked.

"Shouldn't think so. There were nothing in the press. His PA told the papers that he had a lot of money on him, but it was never found," Arthur said.

"Do you know how much money?"

"In the papers it said in excess of half a million," Arthur said. "He was an oddball, was Swan, didn't trust people or banks much. He collected the takings from his shops once a week. That day, his PA reckoned he'd bagged up a fortune."

Jonny scribbled all this down in his notebook. If any of this wasn't in the original murder file, it would need urgent investigation.

"Anything else happen next door?" Jonny asked. "Do you recall anyone who's lived there in the last three years?"

"There was the one that made all the noise," Elsie said. "I remember him, alright. Foul-mouthed he was. It got so bad I gave over speaking to him. It's an unlucky house, that one, there's been nothing but trouble there for years. Thankfully it's empty now, so there's no more noise or strange goings-on."

"Strange goings-on? Can you tell me what you mean, exactly?" asked Jonny.

"That foul-mouthed bugger was there at all times of the day and night. I've no idea what he was doing but the banging got on my nerves," Elsie said. "The walls aren't that thick, so we heard everything. He barely stopped. Arthur here asked him what he was doing and just got a mouthful for his trouble," Elsie said.

"He was converting the cellar into a gym, he told me," Arthur said.

"Was he here at the same time as Swan, the man that died?" asked Jonny.

"No, he was long gone by then."

"If I show you some photos, do you think you'd recognise him?"

"No need, love," Elsie said. "I know him, and where he lives too. He has the pub over by the mill, the Spinners Arms."

Jonny smiled and thanked them. "You've been very helpful. Here's my card. If you think of anything else, just give me a ring."

Back out in the street, Jonny rang the incident room and spoke to Rachel. "The neighbours next door to number forty-five identified Ray Pearce, ma'am. They knew exactly who he was. Pearce must have been the one who opened up the hole down to the tunnel. He made a lot of noise in the cellar, apparently, and disturbed the next-door neighbours. They also told me something else that could be significant. I'll be back in the incident room as soon as."

* * *

Ray Pearce hadn't used much imagination in the alibis he provided for the times Sherwin was killed and Siddall wounded. On both occasions, he insisted he was in the pub. Kath Madison was behind the bar when Amy stopped by.

"How's Rita doing?" Amy asked.

"She's still in hospital. They're trying to decide whether or not she'll need surgery. Is this how it's going to be when she gets home? I wish you lot would leave the poor woman alone. She isn't taking it well, you know. Carry on and it will affect her recovery."

"This isn't about Rita. I'm checking out the alibis Ray has given me for two particular dates." Amy found the details in her notebook and showed her. "Perhaps you can help."

Kath pointed to the date of the night Sherwin was killed. "That's darts match night. He was definitely here then."

"But I'm not sure about the other one," Kath said.

"It would have been during the day," Amy told her. "What does he do when the pub is closed?"

"Goes down the bookies, as a rule. You should ask them."

"The one at the end of the street?"

"Yeah, that and Gladwin's on the main road. He uses them both."

"Does he go anywhere else? Any friends who may be able to vouch for him?"

"No. Ray's a creature of habit. It's the pub or wasting his money on the horses, always has been."

Amy left the pub and went down to the betting shop on the corner. They knew Ray Pearce, and confirmed he was a regular, but said he hadn't been in on the afternoon in question.

"How can you be so sure?" Amy asked.

"Because we were closed, love. That day and the one before, we had no electricity. The box blew. We're lucky the place didn't burn to the ground."

The manager at Gladwin's was more helpful. He also knew Pearce and, after a quick check through his records, was able to confirm that he'd spent all afternoon propping up their counter.

"He won two hundred quid, an amount on one of the early races and some more on a later one, and he placed a number of bets in between."

That meant Pearce's alibis checked out. Amy wasn't looking forward to telling Rachel. A breakthrough was badly needed, and the DCI was losing patience.

CHAPTER FORTY-SEVEN

Rereading statements was not a job Elwyn enjoyed but he had to satisfy himself that he hadn't missed anything. He'd done Siddall's and was ploughing through Rita's when his mobile pinged. It was an email from a bank in Manchester regarding the fifty-pound notes paid to the assault victim, Tunstall, and the fragments found in Wellburn's mouth.

He read it through and could barely believe the words in front of him. He immediately sent the document to the printer, snatched the page and went in search of Rachel. She needed to know at once. This was dynamite.

He found her in the canteen perusing the sandwich counter. "I don't fancy any of them," she said, "but I have to eat something."

"Breakthrough," Elwyn announced. "That cash, the five grand and the notes found in the victim's mouth came from an amount paid out to a bookmaker, one Gordon Swan."

"Do we have any more details? That's not a name that's come up but for some reason it is ringing bells in the back of mind. Do we know who he is?"

"I'm about to go back upstairs and look through the system, see what I can find. This changes things," he said. "I think we can forget the drugs angle."

Rachel nodded. "Get everything you can on this Gordon Swan. We'll have a team briefing shortly."

"Go for the salad," he suggested. "Those chicken ones are past their best."

"I don't fancy lettuce. D'you know what?" She smiled. "I'm going to settle for a bar of chocolate and some crisps."

Elwyn shook his head. "Slippery slope. Think of the little one."

With the new information, it looked as if things were finally moving in the right direction. Elwyn returned to the incident room to find both Jonny and Amy having a quick lunch at their desks.

"I got nowhere with Ray Pearce," Amy told him. "His alibis are sound."

"I've got something interesting. Where's the boss?" Jonny half stood.

"Give her a minute or two. She's grabbing some lunch. How interesting?"

"I had a chat with the people next door to number forty-five, Redhill," he said. "Pearce did the work in the cellar. They remember it well. He made a lot of noise and disturbed the whole street."

"That it?"

"No. Does the name Gordon Swan mean anything to you?" Jonny asked.

* * *

Rachel was about to join the team when she got a call from the front desk. Nell Hennessey was waiting for her in reception. Rachel swore. She'd forgotten again. The woman was becoming a nuisance, particularly as Rachel didn't attach much credibility to what she'd told her so far.

Rachel went down to meet her. "Want to get a drink? The canteen is just through here."

Nell Hennessey nodded and followed in Rachel's wake. "We need to talk. You must tell me everything you can about the young man who approached you."

"He was the same nutcase who stopped me the other night. Tall, young, jazzy trainers. Apart from that, there's nothing to say."

"What did he tell you? Anything different?"

"No. He spouted the same story. I can't believe it. There was an investigation and an inquest at the time — the lot, in fact. I don't know what he hopes to gain. Do you?"

"He wants you onside. It's all part of the scam. He wants you to believe your parents were victims to suit his own ends."

Rachel shook her head. "My parents were not victims, they met with a tragic accident. You can read the reports for yourself, it's all there."

"You don't have to convince me, Rachel," Nell said.

"I don't understand why anyone would think it wasn't an accident. Why would anyone want them dead? They were on a weekend away, at a hotel in Barmouth. There was nothing odd in that. They'd stayed there before. They both liked walking and were doing the Cambrian Coast in stages."

"If the young man contacts you again, let me know at once, Rachel. You aren't the only person he's targeted."

Rachel didn't know what to make of it. She didn't have the time to go into it now, but what Nell was saying made her uneasy. What if the man was right? The thought made Rachel feel sick. If there was any possibility that what had happened to her parents was indeed no accident, it should be investigated.

"Will you help me find this lad, Rachel?"

"I don't know how I can. And anyway, as I said, I'm heavily involved in a murder case of my own at the moment."

"Okay. Once you've done with it, then. I work at the station in Tameside. Join me in a day or so and we'll go through the statements and reports we've gathered so far and take it from there."

Ordinarily Rachel would not have hesitated, but in her present condition, she had other plans. "This isn't common knowledge, Nell, so keep it to yourself. I can't join you, or anyone else for a while. You see, for reasons I won't go into, I'm planning to take extended leave as soon as I've wrapped up this case."

CHAPTER FORTY-EIGHT

Jonny Farrell brought the team up to date with what he'd learned from Arthur Michaels. "It must have been quite something for the people living on that street. Arthur said armed response attended."

"Armed response?" Rachel said. "The neighbours heard shooting?"

Jonny nodded. "They were scared and rang the police, who sent the response team."

"Stella, you looked this one up. Anything odd about the incident?" Rachel asked.

"It was Central that handled it, not us. The information is sketchy, no one was arrested and so the case is still open. Apparently it made all the papers and Swan's family demanded someone be brought to book. But there was nothing to work with, no evidence, only the witness statements from the neighbours which added up to very little. The then SIO has since retired, I'm afraid."

Nonetheless, thought Rachel, it might be worth speaking to whoever that was. "This Gordon Swan. Who was he?"

Elwyn took a page of notes from his desk. "Big-time bookie. Made a fortune but was cavalier about security. He believed he was better off looking after the finances himself, and that included ferrying large amounts of cash all over town."

"So, on this particular day he made his way to Redhill Terrace . . . for what purpose?" Rachel asked. "We could do with finding out."

It was an unlikely scenario. Swan wasn't even local to Ancoats and Redhill Terrace wasn't a street you passed through or would ordinarily even notice.

"Swan was murdered and robbed, ma'am," Jonny said. "Perhaps he was lured to that address."

That could be it. Money belonging to Swan was used to pay off Tunstall, and they knew who was likely to be responsible for that.

"You're thinking that Pearce, Siddall and Wellburn killed Swan?" Elwyn asked.

Rachel nodded. "Given the information we've gathered over the past week or so, I think it's a real possibility. But we need to know more about the incident at Redhill Terrace, and quick. Also, we have no motive, we don't even know if the three knew Swan."

"You could speak to the SIO, see what he has to say," Elwyn suggested.

"Do we know who it was and where they are now?"

"It was a DCI Lennox. After he retired, about a year ago, he moved to Spain with his wife," Elwyn said, reading from the system.

"For now, we'll go with Pearce and Siddall as our main suspects, but Swan may have had other enemies and if so, who are they? I bet that tunnel had something to do with it. Otherwise, why use that particular house? Whoever did him in was familiar with the property and knew about the tunnel. I'd say that has to be why Pearce built an entrance to it from the cellar."

"Do you want Siddall bringing in, ma'am?" Jonny asked.

"Yes, I do. We know the five grand used to pay off Tunstall, and the fragments found in Wellburn's teeth, came from cash the bank paid to Swan. Siddall was party to that assault, same as Pearce."

"We need a time frame for that robbery," Elwyn said. "Swan went to the house, the neighbours heard shots and armed response arrived. They must have been confused when they couldn't find the killer."

"They'll have assumed he got away," Amy said.

"There was CCTV," Jonny told them. "There was no sign of anyone leaving that property. I wonder what they made of it?"

"Well, we know what happened. Swan is shot, the money taken, and the killers scarper down the tunnel."

"I'll be sure to ask Lennox when we speak," Rachel said.

"This murder was planned, given that it takes us back to the same set of names," Elwyn said. "We need to find which one of them hated Swan enough to do that to him."

"Gavin Wellburn worked for a bookie," Amy said. "Perhaps it was Swan. If so, he'd know about his crazy routine with the money."

Rachel nodded. "Check it out. Where was Swan's main office?"

"Salford, ma'am," Amy said.

Rachel considered this. "I'll have a word with Kenton. He might know something about Swan. While I'm gone, find Dylan Healey and we'll have another word with him about Sherwin and the drugs. The drugs element may no longer be relevant but there are still a number of missing pieces in this puzzle."

Rachel gathered up the case notes and made for Kenton's office. He'd worked out of Salford nick for years, so surely, he must know about Swan.

* * *

Rachel entered Kenton's office and sat down opposite him. "Mark, I need a word urgently."

"About the case?" Kenton asked.

196

She nodded. "Gordon Swan. Does the name ring a bell?"

He gave a deep sigh. "It does, and for all the wrong reasons. That man gave me a lot of bother over the years."

"Tell me."

"Is the information relevant to the case? Swan's murder was investigated at the time. I hope you're not considering re-opening that one too."

"No, Mark, just tell me what you know about the man."

"We were continually being called out to incidents at his betting shops. He was a nightmare when it came to security. He dealt only in cash and preferred to look after it himself. He kept the bag he carried the cash in chained to his wrist, silly bugger. He almost lost his hand one afternoon — a gang set about him with a meat cleaver. Fortunately for him, a member of the public rang it in, and we turned up before any damage was done." Kenton shook his head. "That was only one of many times he needed our help."

"Do you know anything about his murder?"

"Not much. Bill Lennox dealt with it. Is this going somewhere, Rachel?

"I need this information, Mark. Just tell me what happened."

"I got involved in the Swan murder because Lennox asked me for advice, me knowing Swan of old. He wanted me to look over the scene."

"Why?" Rachel asked.

"Lennox said it didn't feel right. When he arrived at the house, Swan was lying on the sitting-room floor, a bullet wound in the chest. The bag he carried his money around in, one of those old-fashioned briefcases, was still chained to his wrist, but there was no money in it. What Bill couldn't understand was how the killer got out. No one had left by the front door and it was impossible to get out the back way."

"You do realise which house that is?" Rachel said. "Have you read through the latest reports on the case we're investigating?"

"Not all of them," Kenton said.

"That tunnel we found our body in leads directly to the house on Redhill Terrace where Swan was found. Plus, a victim of an assault carried out by all three of our suspects was paid off using money the bank had issued to Swan. There is a definite link between the cases."

This information appeared to please Kenton. His eyes took on a definite sparkle. "You crack your own case and you might solve this one in the process. That'd be quite a coup for this station. Why don't you speak to Swan's widow, get her take on what happened? She's still around."

That wasn't a bad idea. "How is Bill Lennox likely to react to a phone call from me?" Rachel asked him. "He's not likely to have forgotten, or developed health problems, has he?"

"Bill will be fine. He'll be only too pleased to help. I have his details — I'll email them to you." Kenton smiled.

Progress at last, but Rachel was under no illusions. Kenton was being helpful because he wanted the glory of finally solving Gordon Swan's murder.

CHAPTER FORTY-NINE

Since Ray Pearce was still in the cells, Rachel decided to have another word with him. The noise he'd been making in the house on Redhill had to have been work on the hole leading down into the tunnel.

"Any luck with Healey?" she asked the team. "Pearce, Wellburn and Siddall are almost certainly involved in what happened to Gordon Swan, but I can't work out where Sherwin fits in. Plus, he's only been dealing in the Shawcross area these last couple of years. Prior to that, he wasn't on the scene."

"Not involved, then?" Jonny asked.

"He's involved somewhere. He was shot with the same gun as Wellburn, remember."

Rachel checked her emails. Kenton had already sent through the details for Lennox. It was gone six in the evening — she'd have a drink and grab a bite to eat first and then ring him. "Stella, see if you can find an address for Gordon Swan's wife. We need a word with her urgently."

Rachel went to her office and rang home. Jed answered. "I'm going to be late," she said. "Get Mia sorted, will you? I'll eat something here."

"Don't overdo it, Rachel, it's still early in the pregnancy."

"I'm fine. I'm not doing any physical work, Jed. It's all thinking, figuring stuff out . . . but the case is doing my head in, if I'm honest."

"Okay. Don't stress, we're fine here. Megan's back, she's gone up to her room and doesn't want to join us. Is that down to me, or what?"

"It's just Megan being Megan. She'll have her face buried in that phone of hers. Nothing to do with you."

Rachel hoped she was right, and Megan wasn't having a meltdown. Alan seemed to have gone AWOL with his new woman and Rachel wanted Jed's arrival to be as smooth as possible. But was that asking too much?

When she returned to the office, Stella called to her. "Flora Swan lives in Didsbury, ma'am. I've put her address and phone number on your desk."

"Thanks. I'll ring her in the morning. For now, it's tea, Ray Pearce then a chat with Jim Lennox."

"I'll help with Pearce," Elwyn offered. "He's unpleasant and given to violence."

"He wouldn't dare!" Rachel retorted.

"He's the type that just might. Better not to risk it."

* * *

Elwyn was right. Ray Pearce was furious. He sat facing Rachel and Elwyn, a scowl on his face. "When am I getting out of here?" he demanded. "Wife's in hospital and I've got a pub to run."

"Well, you shouldn't have put her there, Ray. Wrong move that," Rachel said.

He glowered at Rachel, muttering under his breath. "Bloody coppers. This is harassment."

"Tell me about Redhill Terrace, the house you did some work on a few years ago," Rachel said.

Pearce looked stunned. "What d'you mean?"

"It's a simple enough question. We know you rented the place, and the neighbours have told us that you spent all your time working in the cellar."

"I was turning it into a gym."

"Well, there's no gym equipment in there now," Rachel said.

He shrugged. "It was an idea I had. Didn't work out."

Rachel nodded, as if she understood. "Okay, fair enough. So, tell us about the hole you dug that goes down to the tunnel that leads to Shawcross Mill."

"You're mad, you — talking rubbish. What d'you mean, a tunnel? There's no such thing."

"Oh, yes there is, Ray. I've walked it myself."

He grunted. "I need to get home. You've no right keeping me here. I've done nowt."

"You assaulted your wife," Rachel said.

"That was an accident."

"Does the name Gordon Swan mean anything to you?"

Pearce's eyes widened, and he turned to his solicitor. "They're not pinning that one on me. I wasn't involved, none of us were."

Rachel raised her eyebrows. Where had that come from? "Want to explain? 'None of us' — that's a strange thing to say. I presume you're talking about Siddall and Wellburn?"

"No comment. You're getting nothing else from me, copper. I'm likely to get my head blown off."

"Now who would do that? Who are you protecting, Ray?"

He looked down. "No one, figure of speech."

"Why did you think Mathew Shawcross would help you? You wanted to speak to him, remember?"

"I was confused, don't know what I was thinking. That man has never helped anyone but himself. He's a selfish bugger and nasty with it."

"Care to explain?"

"No. Forget what I said."

The problem was Rachel couldn't. Ever since Ray had mentioned his name and she'd gone and spoken to him, Rachel had had a bad feeling about that man.

CHAPTER FIFTY

Rachel and Elwin returned to the incident room. "He's as guilty as sin," Elwyn said. "See his face? He definitely didn't like you bringing Swan up, did he?"

"We still can't prove he dug that hole or who for. He scared to death of someone, but who, Elwyn? We're missing someone in this case. Who is it?" Rachel asked.

"It's too late to think about that now. Time to call it a day. You've got a long drive home."

"I'll speak to Lennox first and then make tracks. You get off," she told him. "You put in the time as well, you know."

He smiled. "But I live a lot nearer to the station."

Rachel said goodnight to Elwyn and went into her office. She dialled Lennox's number and waited.

"Mr Lennox? I'm DCI Rachel King, East Manchester CID. I wonder if you'd mind helping me with some details about an old case of yours."

"No problem, love — if I can."

Rachel smiled to herself. With his broad Northern accent, Jim Lennox sounded friendly enough. "Do you recall the Gordon Swan case?"

"I certainly do. Quite a mystery, that one. Still remains open to this day. During the investigation we spoke to a lot of people, including any number of folk who didn't like the man. But in the end, no one had a strong enough motive to kill him. Then there was the big question of how the killer had got out of the property. CCTV didn't pick anything up and it hadn't been tampered with. We also had statements from a group of kids who'd been in that street all evening. Fair did my head in, that one."

"We have a group of suspects," Rachel told him, "but we're struggling with motive — apart from theft. He was carrying a lot of money, but the suspects in question are certainly not living it up."

"Someone wanted Swan dead, that's for sure. It is likely that he was lured to that address — as far as we could determine, he'd never been there before. I reckoned it was personal. He was planning to divorce his wife, Flora, at the time. Have you spoken to her?" Lennox asked.

"No, but I will," Rachel said. "Do you know why he wanted a divorce?"

"Rumour had it there was another woman, but we never found out who she was."

"Do you know how much money he had on him that day?" she asked.

"His PA said roughly two hundred thousand, but that could have been an exaggeration. He carted it around in bags. One was even chained to his wrist."

"Thank you, Mr Lennox, you've been a great help. We're investigating the Swan case in tandem with another one."

"It's always bothered me. I presumed I'd missed something, had to have, otherwise we would have caught the killer. I mean, we arrived before he left. How could that have been? The neighbours heard the first shot, and forensics later found the bullet buried in the wall. The second shot killed him, and we'd just arrived with armed response. There was just no time for him to make good an escape."

"That property on Redhill Terrace has a secret," Rachel told him. "And that is key to piecing together what happened that night."

"What sort of secret?"

"A tunnel leading from the cellar to Shawcross Mill."

"We had no idea. When it's all over, let me know who you arrest," he said.

"I will," Rachel said, and put down the receiver.

Tomorrow she'd speak to Flora Swan, ask about the woman her husband had planned to leave her for. She ran through the names in her head: Wellburn, Siddall, Pearce. For a while she'd thought there was a fourth — Shawcross, perhaps? But somehow, he didn't fit, not with the likes of Pearce and his cohorts anyway. No, Ray Pearce was a much better bet.

Rachel was out in the corridor, jacket and bag in hand, when she saw the light still on in Kenton's office. She'd have a quick word first.

"Swan's murder is directly linked to that of Wellburn," she told him.

Mark Kenton was watching her closely. "You can prove all this? You have a murder suspect in mind?"

"Yes, but we still don't have definitive proof, Mark. You'll just have to be patient."

CHAPTER FIFTY-ONE

Wednesday

The previous evening, uniform had again arrested Dylan Healey for dealing in Shawcross Mill. He'd been brought in and had spent the night in the cells.

"Want me to interview him?" Jonny asked.

Rachel smiled at the eager young DC. "Yes, see what he has to say about Sherwin. He's a piece of this puzzle that doesn't fit. When you've done with him, bring Siddall in for questioning." She turned to Elwyn. "You and I are off to Didsbury for a word with Flora Swan, Gordon Swan's widow."

Amy looked up from her desk. "I've been checking phone records. Wellburn's provider have finally sent though what I asked for. That number Jonny found on Siddall's mobile — Wellburn rang it too, and there are other numbers. It appears the phone was changed regularly. Whoever used them must have been known to both men, and some of the numbers go back three years."

"Good work, Amy. Get hold of Ray Pearce's records and check them as well."

"You think he rang the same numbers?" Amy asked.

"I'm hoping not. If Pearce is our man, they'll have been burner phones used for incoming calls from the others."

Rachel and Elwyn made for the car. She handed him the keys. "Do you mind driving? I got a printout of the report on Swan's death, and I want to read through it before we tackle Mrs Swan."

"We really need to know who Swan was having an affair with. Jealousy is a strong motive for murder, Rachel."

"Murder and robbery. A lot of money was stolen and that's been bothering me. None of our suspects, not even Ray, have much put away, nor is there any evidence that they spent a great deal in the last three years."

"Siddall bought that bungalow," Elwyn reminded her.

"I got Stella to check. He has a mortgage. Pearce owns the tenancy of that pub, but he took out a bank loan for that years ago. We're missing something, Elwyn. Those three are involved but someone else orchestrated Swan's murder and carried out the shootings."

* * *

They were soon driving into the suburbs at the smarter end of Manchester. Didsbury had a range of small, high-end shops and cafés strung along the high street, followed by leafy lanes with large Edwardian properties. It was a desirable suburb, due to its position well within hailing distance of the city, and the regular tram service made for easy commuting.

"Perhaps we should have told her we were coming," Elwyn said.

"It's better to surprise people. That way, they don't have the opportunity to think too hard about what they're going to tell us. They're inclined to be more truthful."

Flora Swan lived at the head of a wide avenue of impressive detached houses with large front gardens. It was a pleasant, sunny day, and when they parked outside, the detectives saw a woman who had to be Flora pruning roses in the garden.

"Mrs Swan?" Rachel called to her. She flashed her badge. "DCI King and DS Pryce from East Manchester CID. Can we have a word?"

As they approached, Flora Swan's expression hardened. "If it's about that philandering rat of a husband of mine, I've nothing to say." She turned her back and carried on pruning.

"We won't keep you," Elwyn said. "But we do have some questions we need answers to urgently."

She straightened up and stared at them. "Three years, and now suddenly it's urgent! You people amaze me."

"Your husband's murder is linked to a case we are currently investigating. With your help, we may stand a chance of finally charging someone," he said.

The woman didn't look impressed. "Well, I haven't got long."

"We've been looking through the case file," Rachel began. "It seems your husband was having an affair. Do you know who the other woman was?" It was time to be blunt. They needed the truth, not an argument.

"She was deluded. Gordon would never have left me."

"Mrs Swan, her name, please!" Rachel said.

Flora Swan stared away across the garden. "Gordon was complicated, but his head was easily turned by a pretty face, particularly one with a sob story to tell."

"Who are you talking about, Mrs Swan?" Elwyn asked.

Rachel watched the woman wrestle with this. She was on the point of telling them something, but what? "You want his killer caught," Rachel said kindly. "Well, so do we. Help us, tell us what you know. Gordon is dead, there is no longer any reason for you to be embarrassed about his affair."

"I'm not embarrassed, I'm bloody angry! It may be three years down the road, but it still festers. You have no idea what that man put me through. Even today, I still see the pitying looks, hear people whispering. They feel sorry for me and I hate it. That woman would have taken everything — my husband, my home, even my life. The pair of them wanted to throw me on the scrapheap and I couldn't have that."

Rachel had no idea what to make of this venomous outburst. What did she mean? Could she have had a hand in his murder? "You feel aggrieved. I understand that. Want to tell me what you did about it?"

She deflated. "As usual, I did nothing. When it came to it, I bottled out. I didn't even make the phone call."

"What call, Mrs Swan?" Elwyn asked. "It's important that you tell us."

"That woman had a husband, and he was even angrier than I was, if that's possible. He rang me — raging, he was. He told me that he'd make them pay, teach the two of them a lesson, and asked if I would help."

"Did you agree?"

Flora Swan shook her head. "It was a simple enough request, too. All he asked was for me to ring Gordon and tell him to go to a particular address in Ancoats."

"Redhill Terrace." Of course. "Did you know what this man intended to do?"

"No, of course, I didn't, and I didn't make the call either. It was only when Gordon was killed that I realised the man was extremely dangerous and I should have told you lot."

"Do you know his name?" Rachel asked.

"No, and I didn't ask. I didn't want to know anything about him or the woman who'd stolen Gordon from me. I wanted them to remain faceless, nameless. Only then would I stand some chance of forgetting."

"Even so, do you know anything about this woman?" asked Elwyn. "No matter how small, any information you can give us might help."

"No. Nothing. Only that she was divorced from a man who refused to let go and had a daughter who, like me, didn't approve of the relationship."

CHAPTER FIFTY-TWO

Dylan Healey, alias Spider, didn't look happy when he was brought to the interview room.

"Not this again!" Healey said to Jonny. "Don't you lot get fed up with the same old routine? I've done nowt, I know nowt. How many times do I have to say it?"

"Sit still and be quiet, Dylan. You've been dealing again. How many times do you need telling?"

"A bit of weed, nothing heavy. Don't know what all the fuss is about."

"It isn't always just weed though, is it? What about the stuff you sold for Sherwin?" Jonny said.

"What's Sherwin got to do with anything? He's dead, you know that."

"He was shot," Jonny said. "He must have upset someone. You'll have to watch the same doesn't happen to you."

Healey grinned. "Not a chance, mate. I don't mix in the same circles."

"What circles are those?" Jonny asked.

Healey shook his head. "I've said too much already. You're trying to trick me."

"Why would I do that, Dylan? We've told you before, if you're in any danger, tell us and we'll protect you."

"Not from the bastard that got Sherwin you won't." He muttered a curse. "And all because of that stupid girl."

"Jasmine Pearce?"

"No, not her. Some posh bird with a habit. Look, I'm not saying another word. It's too dangerous."

Suddenly it dawned on Jonny. "That posh bird you mentioned. Do you mean Millie Shawcross? We know Sherwin had a hold over her. Her boyfriend, Damon Brooke, is an addict."

Healey's face reddened. "I didn't say that, copper. You can't use it, understand? You didn't hear that off me!"

* * *

Jonny returned to the incident room. Rachel and Elwyn were back.

"Get anything?" Rachel asked him.

"I think Sherwin was killed because of Millie Shawcross. He made her give him that false alibi, remember," Jonny said.

"That brings us back to Damon, her boyfriend, and he has an alibi that's sound," Elwyn said.

"There is someone else who'd be pretty angry at anyone threatening Millie. Her father," Rachel said. She walked over to the board and drew a series of lines connecting some of the names and their photos. "Shawcross is everywhere in this investigation. We need to speak to him again."

"That might be a motive for Sherwin's shooting but what about the others? Swan, for instance?" Elwyn asked. "What connects them all?"

"Is it possible that it was Shawcross's ex-wife that Swan was having the affair with? Shawcross has a reputation for being jealous and controlling." Rachel studied the board, her face thoughtful. "Have him brought in and get a search warrant organised for that mansion of his. Have Jude and her team on standby. We're mainly looking for those burner phones."

Amy put the office phone down. "Andy Siddall has been brought in, ma'am," she said. "We haven't got to the bottom of the phone calls yet. I thought we should ask him outright."

"Did you check out Pearce's records?" Rachel asked.

"Yes, ma'am. He rang the number as well. All the calls the men made follow roughly the same pattern. A lot were on the same dates."

"All three of them then. Who were they speaking to? Shawcross? Come on, Elwyn, we'll go and see what Siddall has to say."

CHAPTER FIFTY-THREE

"How are you doing, Andy?" Rachel asked. "Getting over the attack?"

Andy Siddall nodded.

"It must be tough, knowing that someone wants you dead, yet being unable to give the police a name. But we can help you with that."

"I didn't see his face, just a tall bloke dressed in black with a balaclava over his head. I've no idea who he was," he said.

"I don't believe you, Andy. I think you know very well who shot you, but you're too scared to tell us," Elwyn said.

Rachel watched Siddall closely. He was nervous and he still didn't look well. "You should be in hospital. You discharged yourself against the doctor's advice," she said. "How's Rita? Is she recovering?"

"She had to have surgery. That thug ruptured her spleen."

"You've known Pearce for a long time. You, Ray and Gav were good mates at one time. What happened?" Rachel asked.

Siddall shook his head. "Gav's dead, and me and Ray were never mates in the first place."

"Did you know Gordon Swan?" she said.

Siddall's head shot up. He stared at her. "What's that idiot said?"

"Which idiot do you mean, Ray? No one's told us anything, but we know what happened. We know about the tunnel too."

"Think you've done your homework, don't you?" He gave Rachel a sly smile. "But I'm betting you don't know what it all means. You haven't pieced it together yet or you wouldn't be pumping me for information."

"So, tell us, Andy. Why kill Swan? We've looked at your finances, and you'd didn't benefit from the money that was taken. Tell us who did."

"Can you prove I had anything to do with Swan's murder? No," he stated. "And you won't."

"You're protecting someone. Rita, perhaps?" Rachel asked. "Who from? Ray? Because Ray's locked up in our cells and can't do her any more harm."

"No, not Ray, someone a lot more dangerous who doesn't give a damn who he hurts."

The fourth man. A man who knew Siddall, Pearce and Wellburn, and wielded enough power to make them do his bidding. A man who was so insanely jealous of Gordon Swan he'd been willing to kill him. Shawcross?

"A name, Andy," Rachel said. "Give me a name and we'll arrest him within the hour."

"He'll walk. He has money and power. You'd never make the charges stick. You haven't got enough evidence. I speak to you and I'm dead, and the same goes for Ray. Leave us alone. You'll get nothing from either of us."

* * *

The description Siddall had given was a perfect match for what they knew about Shawcross. But to move the case forward, they needed evidence, badly. Without it, they would never get it past the CPS.

"Get Flora Swan on the phone for me, would you?" Rachel asked Stella. "I'll be in my office."

Leaving Elwyn going through their interview with Siddall and Jonny's interview with Healey, Rachel sat at her desk, her head in her hands. The three men were guilty of something, but murder? She wasn't sure. And if Swan's murder had been down to them, where was the money? Because they certainly hadn't benefitted from it.

Her office phone rang. It was Flora Swan.

"Mrs Swan, I need your help. Try as I might, I can find no evidence against the suspects we're holding for your husband's murder. Is there anything you can tell me that might help?" Rachel asked.

"Gordon got what he deserved. I won't pretend, we'd not been close for ages. He wanted her, he'd even bought her a ring. I never saw it, but I found the receipt in his pocket — Tiffany. Must have cost the old fool a fortune."

Rachel recalled the box found in the tunnel. "You're sure you don't have a name?"

"No. I had no desire then to find out and I haven't now." She was silent for a few moments. "But there was something. I'd forgotten all about it. Me and Gordon were in the middle of a blazing row one evening and his mobile rang. It was her. He became anxious, said he had to go out. His fancy woman had a daughter and she'd got herself drunk and needed picking up. He said he was going out to help find Millie."

CHAPTER FIFTY-FOUR

"We'll speak to Millie. If Swan's girlfriend was her mother, then he was planning to divorce his wife and marry Vanessa Shawcross — or Fenwick, as she was calling herself then. They might have been divorced, but Shawcross wouldn't have been happy with that," Rachel said.

Elwyn nodded. "You're right. Mathew Shawcross is a jealous man. Despite the divorce, he has never relinquished control of his ex-wife and daughter."

"Who can we convince to speak to us first? Pearce or Siddall?" Rachel asked Elwyn

"Siddall might not look it but he's a hard nut. Pearce has a reputation for using his fists. If you ask me, they're just about even."

"Ray Pearce," Rachel decided. "You and me, Elwyn. Cards on the table time. We'll tell him what we know, see if that loosens his tongue. Stella, have him brought up and stick him in interview room three, and get the duty solicitor here quick."

"Ma'am," Amy said, "the last burner phone number was used to call one other mobile apart from the ones belonging to Pearce and Siddall."

"Who did it belong to?" Rachel asked.

"Millie Shawcross, ma'am. The call was made on Saturday."

Rachel turned to Jonny. "Bring her in, and make sure she's got that phone with her. Amy, go with him. Right, come on, Elwyn. Let's get this done with."

* * *

"You and me both know who's responsible for killing Swan and Wellburn, and injuring you. And now I know why," Rachel began.

Andy Siddall said nothing.

"Mathew Shawcross was eaten up with jealousy because his wife was planning to marry Gordon Swan. He concocted a plan to lure Swan to Redhill Terrace. When he got him there, he shot him and stole his money, and then got clean away down that tunnel that leads back to the mill. The police were stumped, no one saw anyone other than Swan enter that house, and they couldn't figure it out."

"Very clever, but you've got no proof. And without that, you've got nothing, only theories," Siddall said.

"So, speak to us, Andy. You don't owe Shawcross anything."

He held up his damaged hand. "Too bloody true I don't. How d'you think I got this?"

"Shawcross?" Rachel shook her head. "In that case, I don't understand why you're protecting him. What's in it for you and Ray Pearce?"

"We get to live."

"He shot you. I'd say the deal was well and truly over. Come on, Andy, level with us. Give us something we can use to arrest Shawcross and make the charges stick." She waited, but he said nothing. "He won't stop, you know. He tried to kill you once and he will try again. You're a target and there's nothing you can do about it."

"I talk and you get Shawcross, me and Ray will be arrested because we helped him," Siddall said.

"Were you there? Did you see Swan shot?"

"No."

"What about Wellburn? Did you witness what happened to him?"

"No."

"In that case, you've nothing to worry about. Help us and we'll help you."

"How do I know I can trust you?" Siddall said. "Whether I speak to you or not, I'll be okay. I plan to leave the area once I know Rita's safe."

"Ray reckons she'll drop all charges and return home to him. We can't hold him for much longer and if Rita doesn't see sense, they'll be together again. You leave and what will she do the next time he thumps her one?"

Rachel watched Siddall wrestle with this. Rita was his one weak point, he'd always done whatever he could to protect her. "Speak to us, Andy, tell us what you know. We'll arrest Shawcross and then you'll all be safe."

"Shawcross deliberately injured my hand to keep me onside. He was proving a point, that he could do much worse if he wanted. He said if I didn't do as I was told I'd lose the use of legs next. He shot Gav because Gav objected to Swan being killed — he used to work for the man at one time.

"Shawcross left him injured, to die alone like an animal. He told me and Ray that if we said anything, we'd get the same treatment. Ray, tough as he is, was terrified, and so was I. You have no idea what a ferocious animal Shawcross is."

Rachel was beginning to appreciate that now. "What happened to the money?"

"Shawcross took it. Swan had a fortune on him. He gave me and Ray twenty grand each and said that meant we were implicated."

"What part did you and Ray play in it all?"

"Ray sorted the access to the tunnel from Redhill Terrace and we both helped to clear the route. That tunnel needed digging out in parts. It must have been flooded at some time

— the mud and silt made walking through it impossible. Shawcross wouldn't tell us why he wanted it cleared."

"What about the night Swan was killed?" she asked.

"Ray was in the pub and I was in hospital with my hand. Me and Shawcross had argued two days previous, and he took a lump hammer to it."

Rachel winced. "I want a comprehensive statement from you. I will speak to Ray and urge him to see sense too."

"And Shawcross?"

"He will be arrested and questioned."

Siddall shook his head. "He'll deny everything."

Rachel looked at him. "You'll have to trust me, Andy. I meant it when I said we'd get him. And the charges will stick."

CHAPTER FIFTY-FIVE

"Sorry to disturb you, Millie, but would you mind coming with us?" Jonny asked.

"Why, Jonno? What for? I've done nothing wrong," Millie said.

Amy stifled a giggle. Jonny'd had it now, the nickname was out.

"Can I ring Damon?" Millie asked.

"Yes, of course, bring your phone," Jonny said, still red in the face. "You're not under arrest, we just want you to answer a few questions at the station."

Amy could see that Millie was nervous. If they wanted her to talk to them, a friendly approach was needed. "Nice place you have," she said. "Handy for the city."

Millie smiled. "It's looking a bit more like home now I've got some of my own stuff about the place."

Amy looked around. She could see that the girl had spent money on the place. Her gaze fell on a photo adorning the mantelpiece. It showed Millie with her father and a woman she took to be her mother. "Happy families?"

"Definitely not. When that was taken, my parents were at war and I was piggy in the middle. Believe it or not, that was taken three years ago on my dad's forty-fifth birthday. Later that same day, me and mum left him."

Amy picked up the framed photo and studied it. Vanessa Shawcross did look pensive, but Mathew looked happy enough. And there was something else. "That Saint Christopher pendant he's wearing. Was it a birthday present?" Amy squinted at the photo. Yes, it looked just like the Saint Christopher she'd been researching.

"Yes, from me. He can't have thought much of it though. Within days he'd lost it. The thing never did turn up."

"Where did you buy it, Amy?" Jonny asked.

"That jewellers on Market Street, the one near the sports shop. It was gold, expensive — not that my dad was impressed."

Amy smiled. "Nice present. Shame to lose it."

They escorted Millie outside to the car.

* * *

Rachel suspected that Shawcross had killed Sherwin because he was threatening his daughter. She was hoping that Millie could tell her something that would help. She didn't want the young woman on the defensive, so easy does it was the way to go.

Rachel entered the interview room with a smile on her face. "Can we get you something, Millie? Coffee, perhaps?"

"I'm fine, thanks. Let's just get this done," Millie said.

"Could I have a look at your mobile phone?" Rachel asked.

Without a word, Millie slid it across the table.

Rachel flipped through the call log until she found it — an incoming call from an unknown caller on Saturday. "Who was this?"

Millie took her phone back and looked. "My dad. He rang me from his spare mobile."

"Does he do that often?"

"No, but he was out and had forgotten his own. He used an old one he found in his car."

"What did he want?"

"He asked me if I was okay, said I wasn't to worry any more about the trouble Damon had got himself into."

"May I keep your phone for a while?" Rachel asked.

Millie looked doubtful. "I suppose so. Will I get it back?"

"Yes. We won't keep it for long." Rachel smiled. "I'll get someone to run you home."

* * *

Back in the incident room, Rachel rang the tech department. "I'm emailing you a mobile number. I want to know what masts it pinged on Saturday afternoon — and it's urgent, I'm afraid."

She turned to the team. "Shawcross killed Sherwin and then rang his daughter from his latest burner phone. If we get proof of this from the tech boys, then we've got him."

"There's a photo in Millie's flat of her father wearing that Saint Christopher that was found with Wellburn's body," Amy told her. "Jude will test Shawcross's DNA against what they found on it."

"Good work, Amy, well spotted. If the DNA checks out, we can put Shawcross in that tunnel — along with Wellburn."

"I've had a call from the two officers who arrested him," Elwyn said. "Shawcross put up a fight — raging at them with his fists, Constable Hamilton reported."

"In that case we'll interview him mob-handed — you, me, two PCs and a couple more outside the door."

CHAPTER FIFTY-SIX

When Rachel and Elwyn entered the interview room, Shawcross was talking quietly with his solicitor. He smiled at the officers as they took their places.

"This is a waste of time," he said evenly. "I haven't done anything. I have no idea why you've brought me here."

"You are here to answer questions about the murders of Gordon Swan, Billy Sherwin and the malicious wounding of Andy Siddall." Rachel smiled.

Shawcross said nothing, merely sat and stared at Rachel as if she was mad.

"Tell me about Gordon Swan," she went on. "Despite not knowing the man, you didn't like him much, did you?"

"As you say, I didn't know him, therefore I had no opinion of him one way or the other. He was a bookmaker, I believe. I've seen his shops all over town, and in Salford."

"He was having an affair with your ex-wife," Rachel said.

He stared at her with his eyes narrowed. "You're wrong. Vanessa wasn't interested in him."

She shook her head. "Not true. They were about to become engaged."

Shawcross slammed his fist on the desk. "No! Vanessa and me were getting together again. What happened between us was just a blip."

"You were jealous. You wanted to get even, get rid of the man. That's the truth of the matter, isn't it?"

"You're wrong. This is wildly out of line. I would never harm anyone!"

"You harmed Andy Siddall," Rachel said. "You destroyed his hand — deliberately, he told me."

"He's lying."

"Billy Sherwin, the drug dealer, you shot him because he was threatening your daughter." Rachel paused. "I see a pattern here, Mr Shawcross. I see people dying and suffering because of your uncontrollable jealousy."

"Wrong!" He turned to his solicitor. "Tell her, Rafe, tell her I would never do the things she's accusing me of."

"Do you have evidence of my client's guilt?" the solicitor asked. "Because if you don't, this is just a waste of all our time."

Rachel swallowed. She knew they'd have to wait a while for the DNA from the Saint Christopher to be matched to that of Shawcross. But the tech people might have something on the phone. Rachel stood up, gathered her paperwork and made for the door. "I'll give you a few minutes to consider your position."

Outside in the corridor, she inhaled deeply. "He's giving nothing away, Elwyn. We need that evidence and quick. There's no way I want Shawcross walking out of here." She shook her head. "Even if we do get what we need, there is nothing that links him to Gordon Swan's murder except knowledge of that tunnel and intense jealousy. Not enough. We need more."

"Dr Glover wants a word," Jonny told her.

Heart racing, Rachel dialled the lab. The right result was vital.

"It's good news, Rachel. The blood we found on Sherwin's knuckles matches with the DNA we found on the Saint Christopher."

"So, whoever owned that pendant was in Sherwin's flat?" Rachel asked.

"Yes, so the pendant had to belong to the killer, not Wellburn, like we thought originally."

"I need the result for Shawcross quickly, Jude. I'm hoping it matches with what you've found."

"We're working on it. I'll be in touch. I dug out the forensic evidence from the Gordon Swan case. The bullet that killed him is a match for the ones that killed Wellburn and Sherwin."

"The same gun?"

"Yes, Rachel. Finding it is high on the list."

"Email from communications, ma'am," Amy said. "The call the burner phone made to Millie Shawcross on Saturday pinged a mast by Billie Sherwin's Ardwick flat."

That meant Shawcross must have been there. "Has the search of his home turned up anything?" Rachel asked.

"They're still looking."

"Rachel, take a break," Elwyn said. "You look tired. Have a bite to eat and a sit down."

Rachel had to admit that she didn't feel quite right — she was dizzy for a start. But there was no way she could leave yet. "Once those phones are found, get them to the lab. Jude will check for Shawcross's DNA."

One of the uniforms from the interview room wanted a word with Rachel. "His solicitor isn't happy, ma'am. He wants to know what evidence we've got. If there's nothing, Shawcross wants releasing at once."

Rachel had heard enough. The man was a killer and he would get what was coming to him. "Elwyn, with me."

Rachel strode into the interview room and faced the pair. "Before the day is over, Mr Shawcross, you will be charged with murder. The evidence is building."

"This is ridiculous. I can't sit around here. I need to get home."

"No way. You will be spending the night in the cells."

"On what evidence?" he asked.

"For starters, we can prove you were in Billy Sherwin's building the afternoon he was killed. He hit you, didn't he? We found traces of blood on his knuckles that did not belong to him. What's the betting that it's a match to your DNA?"

Rachel watched his face redden. He was barely controlling his rage. "Not only that, we found the Saint Christopher pendant your daughter bought you. It was with the body of Gavin Wellburn. Do you want me to go on?"

The solicitor started to pack up his things. He saw the way things were going. "I'm sorry, Mathew. I'll be back in the morning. We'll discuss your position then."

"I'm innocent, Rafe. Don't go believing her. She's got no idea."

CHAPTER FIFTY-SEVEN

Thursday

Rachel took the morning off. She had her scan appointment, which was a big event for both her and Jed. The sonographer confirmed Rachel's due date, but much to Jed's disappointment, it was too early to tell if it was a girl or a boy. Jed wanted a boy. Rachel wasn't bothered, but after raising two girls, she did think a boy would be a nice change.

She'd rung the station and they confirmed all was well. Shawcross had seen his solicitor and was a lot quieter. It seemed some good advice had been doled out.

"When are you giving up the job?" Jed asked when she'd finished the call. "You need to rest, and we've got to plan what we're doing with the houses."

"Who says we're doing anything with them and who are you to tell me to rest? I like my house just as it is, thank you."

"We could knock them together, make a bigger living space for the kids."

It was a wonderful idea, but Rachel wasn't sure if she wanted to take it on. "Think of the mess, the upset of having workmen all over the place. This baby will be here in less than six months. It's a lot to take on."

"You forget, I know people in the trade. I could have it done and dusted within a couple of months. We already have the plans — Alan drew them up, remember?"

Alan had had big plans too, and look what had happened there. "It's not just about the house, though, is it?" she said. "There's us to consider, and the sort of relationship we'll have."

"No problem on my part. I want to marry you."

That threw her. "I can't talk about this now. I need to go to work, check how the team are doing. Let's not hurry the marriage thing, it's too soon. I want the girls to get used to having you around before we do anything so rash. And I haven't had a proper conversation with Alan yet."

"Alan will be fine, he's got the Belinda on his arm and the pair of you are divorced," he reminded her. "As for the girls, they're growing up fast. Megan is already living part-time with her friend and Mia doesn't have a problem with me at all."

"I'll consider everything, and we'll talk about our future together another time."

* * *

Friday

Superintendent Mark Kenton was sitting at Rachel's desk waiting for her when she arrived.

"I've heard an unsettling rumour," he said.

"Not about the Shawcross case. That's doing fine, thank you."

"No, about you. A little bird tells me you're planning on taking extended leave."

Now, who . . . ? Not Elwyn, he'd promised to keep quiet, and she trusted him absolutely, so who'd ratted on her?

Then it dawned. "Nell Hennessey. I had to tell her something to get her off my back." Her voice sounded too high-pitched, even to herself. Kenton knew she was lying.

"Are you planning to leave us, Rachel? Straight answer. I know I pointed out those jobs in Stockport, but I wasn't being serious. I don't want to lose you," Kenton said.

"Even though I'm stubborn and bloody expensive on the forensics front? Are you sure, Mark?"

"Your team is doing a good job. I've no complaints. Come on, what is this rumour all about?"

Rachel poured herself an orange juice from a carton she'd brought in. "I'm pregnant, Mark, just over three months."

Kenton stared at her as if he hadn't heard her right. "You sure?"

"Quite sure. I've trodden this path before. And before you ask, yes, Jed is the father."

He coughed. "What's next with Shawcross? Got all the results you need yet?"

Rachel smiled. Prefer to ignore the bit about Jed, did he? "I'll check in with Jude shortly. But he isn't going anywhere, our guest. He's as guilty as sin."

Kenton picked up his mobile and started to scroll through the images. "Evidence that he killed Swan is a bit thin, circumstantial in the main. Perhaps this will help."

Rachel took the device from him. The photo showed the body of Swan lying in the sitting room of Redhill Terrace.

"Where did you get this?"

"It was sent by Shawcross to his ex-wife Vanessa on the night he shot Swan. It was meant as a warning. She did nothing about it — too afraid. She knows Shawcross of old. But she had the foresight to keep it, just in case. I've sent it to the IT technicians. They can give you the date of when it was taken."

"This is great, Mark, just what we need. Shame the woman didn't give us this sooner."

"She's terrified of him, Rachel. Which is why she has avoided coming to see us during this investigation. If Shawcross had the merest hint that Vanessa was helping us, he'd have killed her." Kenton got up to leave.

"He definitely won't wriggle out of this one now," she said. "I can't wait to see his face."

"We'll miss you," Kenton said, "but you will come back, won't you? You're not thinking of leaving us for good?"

"I'm not sure what I'm thinking, Mark. Jed wants to marry me. If that happens, it'll change both our lives."

She was winding Kenton up. Rachel was a long way off deciding about marriage. She'd tried it once and it hadn't worked, so why go through it again?

Her office phone rang. It was Jude, calling from the lab.

"It's good news, Rachel, the best. The DNA from the blood on Sherwin's hand and the Saint Christopher match that of Mathew Shawcross. It looks like you've got him."

The icing on the cake. Rachel heaved a sigh of relief. There was no way he could argue, scream or fight his way out of this one. He'd killed three men, and injured Siddall twice. Shawcross was going down for a long time.

EPILOGUE

Three months later

"Look at you!" Amy exclaimed as Rachel entered the office. "You're positively blooming. Pregnancy suits you, ma'am."

Rachel ran a hand over her baby bump. "Thanks. I think I'm quite enjoying the whole experience this time round."

"You heard about Shawcross?" Elwyn asked.

"Yes, it was in the papers. I would never have had him down as the suicidal type," Rachel said.

"Hanged himself with a ripped-up bedsheet," Amy said.

Elwyn handed her a drink. "The CPS are still deciding what to do about Siddall and Pearce. Siddall is just getting on with his life, but Pearce has been knocking Rita about again. She's decided to press charges this time. So, we'll wait and see."

Rachel's eyes strayed to her office. "Replaced me yet? I did hear something."

Elwyn smiled. "She starts Monday, and I'm sure she's not a patch on you."

"According to her reputation she is, if not better. Nell Hennessey is an excellent detective. Give her a chance, Elwyn."

"She's bringing her own sergeant with her, a DS Rio Sharpe. I don't even know if that's a man or a woman's name. What d'you think?"

"Rio is a young woman, tipped to go far. Nell took her under her wing a couple of years ago. She was a DC back then."

"It still won't be the same," Jonny said. "You will come back to us, won't you? Once the baby comes, you won't decide to leave or anything?"

Rachel laughed. "You will all be just fine without me. Do your best. Impress DCI Hennessey and you'll make DS in no time."

Rachel went around the team one by one, hugging them goodbye. "You're all invited to the christening. In the meantime, be good, and don't upset the new boss too much. See you all later."

Rachel left the office with tears in her eyes. She'd never imagined the day would come when she'd walk away from the job she loved. But Jed and the baby, the pull they had on her heartstrings, had won for now.

THE END

ALSO BY HELEN H. DURRANT

DETECTIVE RACHEL KING
Book 1: NEXT VICTIM
Book 2: TWO VICTIMS
Book 3: WRONG VICTIM
Book 4: FORGOTTEN VICTIM

THE DCI GRECO BOOKS
Book 1: DARK MURDER
Book 2: DARK HOUSES
Book 3: DARK TRADE
Book 4: DARK ANGEL

THE CALLADINE & BAYLISS MYSTERY SERIES
Book 1: DEAD WRONG
Book 2: DEAD SILENT
Book 3: DEAD LIST
Book 4: DEAD LOST
Book 5: DEAD & BURIED
Book 6: DEAD NASTY
Book 7: DEAD JEALOUS
Book 8: DEAD BAD
Book 9: DEAD GUILTY
Book 10: DEAD WICKED

DETECTIVE MATT BRINDLE
Book 1: HIS THIRD VICTIM
Book 2: THE OTHER VICTIM

DETECTIVES LENNOX & WILDE
Book 1: THE GUILTY MAN

Please join our mailing list for free Kindle crime thriller, detective, mystery and romance books, and new releases!

www.joffebooks.com

Made in the USA
Las Vegas, NV
22 January 2021